One

Summer

by

Albert Drake

Flat Out Press

The author is grateful to the editors of the following magazines who have previously published sections of this novel (sometimes in earlier forms): *Assembling, Center, Cloud Chamber, Cream* City *Review, First Person Intense* (Mudborn Press), *Gargoyle, Graffiti, Happiness Holding Tank, King Johns Version, The Mill, New Rivers Review, Northwoods' Journal, Rockbottom, The Smith, The Smudge; Spectacle, Wind.*

He is also grateful for a National Endowment for the Arts Fiction Fellowship and a Michigan State University Faculty grant which allowed time for the novel to be written.

ISBN-13: 978-0936892245
Library of Congress
Cataloging in Publication No.: 79-63672

Originally Published by:
The White Ewe Press

Second Edition by:
Flat Out Press
PO Box 66874
Portland, OR 97290-6874

www.flatoutpress.com

For my mother, Hildah, who got me here,
and my sister, Bonnie, who gave me a typewriter

Contents

Legend

1. Chris's House
2. Hideout in the fields of Scotch Broom & Oregon Grape
3. Horace's house
4. Site of the Epic Battle
5. Area of the jockey-boxing
6. Orlando's Store
7. The Path
8. The Old Lents School
9. Mac's Grocery
10. The House That Burned
11. The Branch Where Chris disposed of the ground squirrels
12. Merhar's Drive-inn
13. Lents Proper: The intersection of streets & lives
14. The Lents Evangelical United Brethren Church
15. PGE Substation
16. Where Chris smoked the cigarette
17. Where Chris & Horace made the sacrificial offering to the Goose
18. Dwyer's Mill
19. 112th St. Hill: Site of the Great Soapbox Race
20. The reservoir in the cemetery
21. Where Chris shot the weasel
22. The Vision happened here

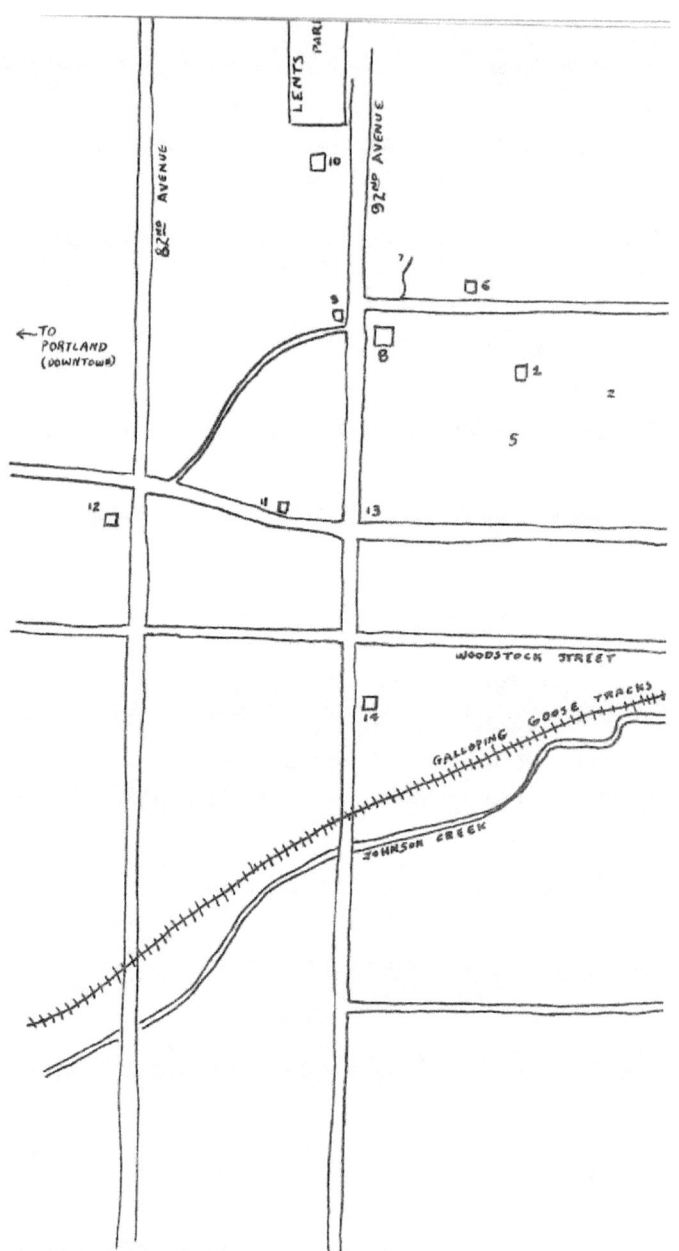

LENTS PARK

82ND AVENUE

92ND AVENUE

← TO
PORTLAND
(DOWNTOWN)

10

7

6

9

8

1

2

5

12

11

13

WOODSTOCK STREET

14

GALLOPING GOOSE TRACKS

JOHNSON CREEK

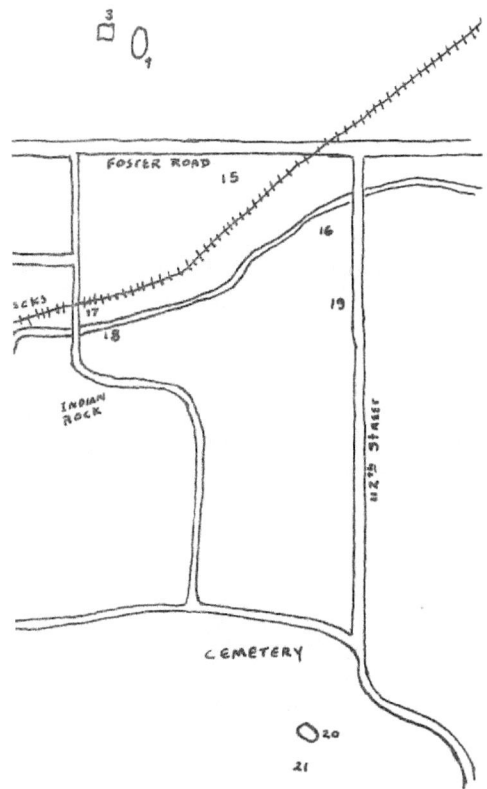

N

TO GRESHAM ⟶

HAROLD STREET

3

9

FOSTER ROAD

15

16

19

SCRS

17

18

INDIAN
ROCK

112th STREET

CEMETERY

20

21

LOST
LAKE

MT. SCOTT

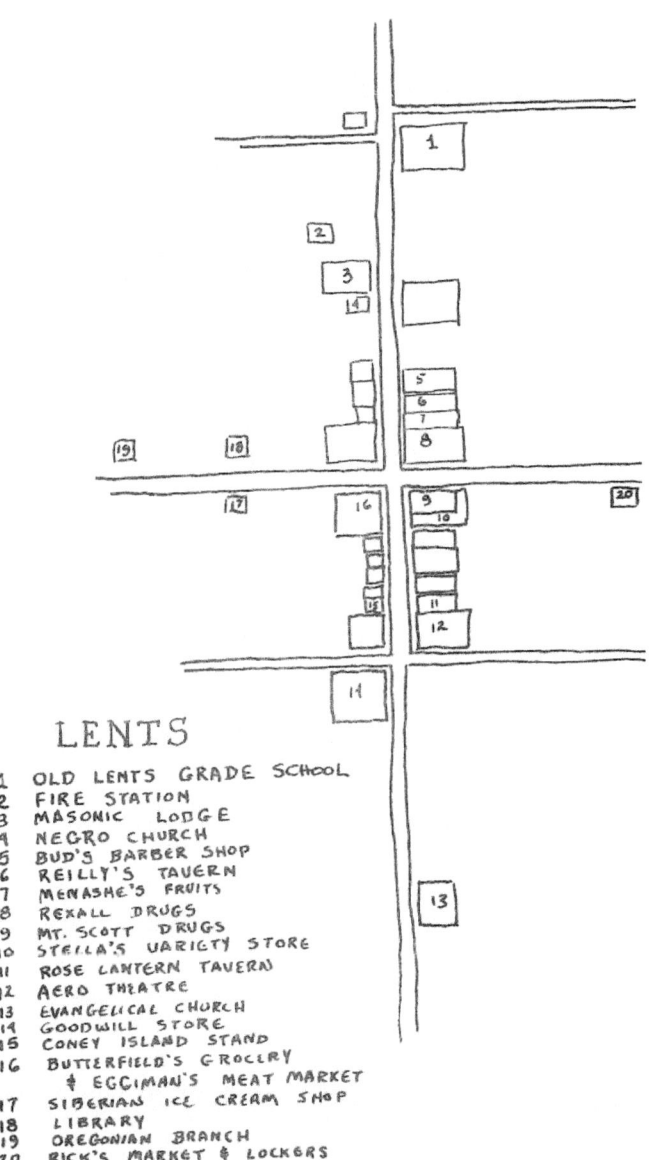

LENTS

1 OLD LENTS GRADE SCHOOL
2 FIRE STATION
3 MASONIC LODGE
4 NEGRO CHURCH
5 BUD'S BARBER SHOP
6 REILLY'S TAVERN
7 MENASHE'S FRUITS
8 REXALL DRUGS
9 MT. SCOTT DRUGS
10 STELLA'S VARIETY STORE
11 ROSE LANTERN TAVERN
12 AERO THEATRE
13 EVANGELICAL CHURCH
14 GOODWILL STORE
15 CONEY ISLAND STAND
16 BUTTERFIELD'S GROCERY
   & EGGIMAN'S MEAT MARKET
17 SIBERIAN ICE CREAM SHOP
18 LIBRARY
19 OREGONIAN BRANCH
20 RICK'S MARKET & LOCKERS

Waking

The rhythm of Chris's breathing was deep and easy; the cool late spring air was inhaled and held, and sometime later with an imperceptible sound it was exhaled. His face beneath the tousled hair was soft, peaceful, unlined except for the sfumato areas where lips had pulled into a slight smile, as if he heard an internal radio program falling on the mind like a handful of notes from a popular love tune. He had lain motionless in deep, untroubled sleep for hours, but now his lips moved into a smile, as if he had just thought of something funny or pleasurable.

In the backyard the willow shook its leaves; they danced like pale yellow fish. Random low clouds, like those in comic strips, scudded toward the east at what seemed rooftop level; beyond, the sky was a deep blue lightened with a full moon and a galaxy of stars. The breeze through the open window carried scents of the tactile, physical world, of cut grass and lilac, cedar and Japanese plum, laurel and geranium, mountain ash and Oregon Grape and Scotch Broom and the cool wetness of sprinklers: perhaps these wind-borne stimuli evoked that smile of pleasure.

It was the kind of night one hates to waste on sleep: the dirt breathed small breaths, glass glowed, the big rock under the outside water faucet seemed to radiate kryptonite, clothes flapped on the line whiter than they would ever be in daylight. With every house in the neighborhood dark, nothing was brighter than the moon's pale light. It had rolled over the tips of the Cascades, topped Mt. Hood, and then moved slowly through the branches of the Japanese Plum tree beside the driveway and over the neighbor's house, where the roofline cut it like a diagram. Now it hovered slightly past the median of night, as full and as white as the exaggerated, stylized moon which characterizes the city skyscapes in the Sunday funnies; the terrain of its milky surface was broken only by the small bluish areas, like bruises.

It was the kind of night which affirms the joy of living, but few were awake to experience this affirmation. Lents was nearly empty. The clean-up man in Reilly's Tavern swept cigarette butts,

1

broken glass, and Sen-Sen wrappers toward the door. Tonight the Aero Theater had had only a handful of patrons and so Bratt, the owner, had gone home without sweeping all that empty space. Eggiman's Meat Market and the adjacent Butterfield's Grocery were dark except for a single dim night light. The Goodwill store slept with secondhand ghosts. Neon signs flickered in the windows of the Mt. Scott and Rexall drugstores like trapped insects. All the other stores were dark and empty beneath awnings which were pulled like bedrolls tightly against the battered walls.

At the intersection of 92nd and Foster the stop light flashed like a beacon warning of some remote point of land. No cars had been along either street for almost an hour. The streets were empty in all directions except for the two cars by the Rose Lantern, left by drunks who had found other transportation or who were perhaps sleeping in the cars' back seats.

Like an apparition, a figure came from the alley near the hardware store and stumbled off in the general direction of the Rexall. It was Old Man Mountain, burdened by a gunny sack slung over his shoulder, eyes concentrating on the sidewalk as if it might get away from him.

Under the shadow of Mt. Scott, Lents slept. The only movement anywhere was the tallow-yellow light of the Galloping Goose, the inter-urban trolley, as it clattered steel on steel and hooted its mournful signal at the 103rd Street crossing and disappeared into the darkness toward Gresham. The breeze stirred the air, moving limbs, which was like a pebble disturbing still water. Overhead the night sky moved like a ship with a million portholes. Each tiny maroon Japanese plum reflected moonlight.

Chris smiled as he dreamed, collecting possible images of himself walking along the rimrock at White River hunting ground squirrels, and camping on Mt. Scott, and going downtown with Horace, and stealing homemade pickles from back porches with Mal, and riding his bike on the trails that intersected Indian Rock, and shooting off fireworks and going to the movies and picking berries and doing his paper route and sitting in the

2

coolness of the Rexall slowly spooning the ice cream from a deep-throated soda glass while he read a comic and lying in the hammock *and everything's possible!* he felt on an inarticulate level beyond thought which did not need to be thought or perhaps couldn't be. Not memory but anticipation supplied the images. They piled up frame after frame like comic strips laid together but without order or priority, each frame having a meaning and not necessarily dependent upon another frame even as a point of reference.

Later, dew collected along the surfaces of leaves and grass, descending with the coolness of a membrane. In the fields across the street spider webs strung between grass stalks were etched with dew. Down the block a dog barked, and from far away came an answering howl. In darkness birds began to wake noisily and before the first light of false dawn masses of robins and sparrows moved from tree to tree and perched like the repetition of a single note along the telephone wires.

Along the edges of the Cascades the sky was tinged a bright red, which merged upward to yellow and an intense blue; the north side of Mt. Scott was bright with sunlight while Lents lay in shadow. A rooster gave a long, defiant crow, repeated at regular intervals; soon fifty roosters answered in a cacophony of communication.

Pipes rattled within walls, a toilet flushed, dishes banged together. A screen door closed and after a pause his father's car door slammed; the starter ground, the engine caught, warmed, was driven to work. Other cars were driven along the street, the exhaust piping condensation into the cool morning.

Through these sounds he slept, dimly aware of the birds, dogs, roosters, traffic; he pulled the covers over his ears and retreated into sleep. He finally woke to a sound like *ziiiip,* as though a big zipper were being pulled quickly underwater. Chris opened his eyes and looked around, saw sunlight coming through the burlap curtains, shining on the guns on his walls, and realized two things: the strange sound he had heard was water from the hose which his mother was playing across the screen on his window, and he also realized: no school!

He shook sleep from his eyes, suddenly aware that now he was done with grade school as of yesterday, and done with all school for three months. He was free, unfettered, could do anything but did not have to do anything: as he lay back on the pillow and closed his eyes the sense of freedom came in the form of unexposed film upon which the images could be developed, but this idea came on the subliminal level near the unspoken feeling that *everything's possible! everything's possible!* which he felt as a joyous celebration coursed along his skin, a supercharged energy which drove away sleep, but which he could not articulate only demonstrate.

His Room

The room was an addition his father had built to the garage, and, since it was not connected to the house, within its walls Chris felt secure and independent. It was a fort, hunting lodge, and sanctuary.

The walls held his weapon collection: several rifles, a shotgun, a Civil War cavalry saber, a bow and quiver of arrows, a machete, a WW II Japanese rifle and bayonet, various knives. There were old display cards of Indian and Lincoln head pennies and Mercury dimes.

The bookcase–several wooden apple boxes–held his best books: *Fighting Man* by Max Brand, *I Escaped From Devil's Island* by Rene Beloit, *Bugles in the Afternoon* by Ernest Haycox, *Little Caesar* by W.R. Burnett, *Over the Top* by Capt. McBride, *The Lost God* by John Russell, *Beau Geste, Jesse James was My Neighbor, They Died with Their Boots On,* and a dozen others. There were stacks of *Amazing, Astounding,* and *Fantastic* pulps, *True* and *Argosy, Blue Book* and *Esquire.*

Cardboard boxes of comic books towered in one corner.

While his friends would read a comic once and throw it away, he saved them all. *Walt Disney, Crime Does Not Pay, Airboy, Daredevil, True Comics, Plastic Man, Blue Beetle, Boy, Supersnipe, Jingle-Jangle Tales,* and hundreds of others. Once a year he would read through the piles; they were like old friends.

He collected everything. He saved baseball cards (although he disliked baseball), Pep cereal pins, matchbooks, military patches, newspaper photos of western singers, race car drivers, and automobiles. He saved radio programs, American and foreign coins, bullets, cartridges, boxtop specials, western and hillbilly records. Also dice, marbles, gear-shift knobs, Buick hood ornaments, old rocks, stamps, books, deer antlers, and, in a tiny film viewer, all of his baby teeth. He collected the days in his diary.

Idling

He pumped slowly, feeling good in the sun. His spokes clicked past the point where the street ended, just beyond his house, and the oiled gravel became dirt. Twin ruts ran unevenly toward the east. He had owned the bike for so long that it had become an extension of his body, and together they knew every rough spot on the road.

Theirs was the last house; beyond lay fields of Scotch Broom and high grass. Here they had played war, crawling through the system of foxholes and trenches; they had hunted garter snakes, filled jars with grasshoppers. On certain Saturday mornings the fields glistened with a misty haze; all colors were greenish brown, like ripening hazel nuts.

Today it was pleasantly warm, the fields were a brilliant green, and he rode easily over the bumps. He gripped the wide handlebars, felt the wind lift his hair; over the ruts the bike rose and fell, kicking up a thin plume of dust. Above the gently waving grass he could see the confusion of Scotch Broom, and beyond it, to the south, was Mt. Scott. To the east were the Cascades, and directly ahead Mt. Hood towered. His father said he was far-sighted: "I can stand out front and see all the way to Mt. Hood."

Chris knew that the street and the city ended in marshy fields a few blocks away, but he knew if the road were continuous it would lead directly to the mountain. He thought he would like to try that ride one of these days.

Feeling Good

He felt good riding his bike, listening to the radio, hanging around Lents, reading books, waking in the morning, listening to the stories that his imagination described as boundless. He felt excitement, joy, wonder, the thrill of the world that unfolded around him. Hardly ever did he not feel good.

He liked to wake and pull aside the curtain, to investigate the day; he liked to walk out of the house into whatever weather. On some days there was a tinge of greenness in the air, as if it had travelled through groves of wet, young trees; other days the way the smoke rose from neighboring houses, the smell of burning wood, excited him. On Saturday mornings he would wake early, get a stack of comic books from the boxes and an orange, or his mother would bring him cocoa and toast, and he would turn on the radio: Let's Pretend, The Buster Brown Show, Grand Central Station, The Explorer's Club. Then he and Horace would head for town.

Sunday mornings were slower: his parents slept in; the streets were silent except for the bark of a lone dog or the crow of a distant rooster. Because there were only church programs on the radio, he would lie in bed and reflect on the past or future. In a recurrent image he saw himself waking as a young boy, climbing into the warm bed with his sleeping parents, and drawing pictures in a linen tablet while the radio quietly played "My Adobe Hacienda" and rain gently dripped from the eaves. The image was so distant he could see the texture of the paper, and the way the rain drops ran together before falling.

He liked to go to the Aero on a weeknight, when the building was almost empty. When he left, he walked close to the walls and hedges, playing the film in his head. Because films came to the places on Broadway first, slowly working their way outward to the suburban theaters, and came to the Aero last, Chris imagined that every film was kept in a small room in the back; he dreamed of being allowed to enter that room and pick out his favorite films for additional showings.

6

But he also enjoyed going to the big theaters downtown: the wide stairways, the larger screen, the several balconies, the overwhelming odor of butter-rich popcorn, the intricate detail work of the dome which was the roof, the glare of lights and traffic when he stepped blinking onto the sidewalk after a lengthy double-feature.

He liked to ride his Western Flyer on the hills in Lents Park, or on the sidewalks of Lents, to idle along watching the fat tire whizz over the ribbed cement. Or to ride the motorcycle trails of Indian Rock, imagining that the bike did indeed have an engine.

He liked to haul a box of comic books into the backyard, climb into the hammock, and spend the afternoon nibbling potato chips and lingering over the smell of old paper.

Often he felt the need to be alone, as if isolation was a blanket he could pull around himself. He liked to stand in the middle of the new room his father had built for him, the curtains drawn, the walls covered with his very own weapons and maps and books. Or to go into the garage, to stand in the cavernous dark space and look through old cigar boxes filled with junk—his father's union pins, watch fobs, spark plugs, brass fittings, dashboard knobs, pipes—or to simply sit on an empty nail keg and think about things. He liked to stand under a towering fir at the edge of the treeline on Mt. Scott, studying the city which spread out before him, and he especially enjoyed this on a rainy day when the low clouds moved like slow ghosts across the mountainside, the boughs collecting the rain. At such moments he felt like the only person on earth, and the thought would send a chill along his spine.

He liked to lie in bed at the end of a long day, the house darkened, the wall of his room faintly illuminated by the orange glow of his radio's tubes. The voice from the radio was comforting to him, a disembodied companion, and as the lights in the adjoining houses flickered and died, when there were only the neighborhood arc lights, he appreciated this kinship. The drama programs ended at ten, and then he listened to the news, amazed at everything that went on in the world. All of those lives, people doing things, and yet their lives had little or nothing to do with his own, he thought. On Sunday nights after the news came a program called Down Memory Lane which made him feel funny. The announcer claimed to be sitting in a rocking chair beside a fireplace, a spinning wheel nearby, and he was playing once again the old favorites. Chris would stare at the patterns on the ceiling, feel himself transported in those moments before sleep back in time, among people who seemed more real than his contemporaries.

Lost Lake

Early, under a dull, leaden-gray sky, he walked for the last time the familiar blocks to Lents' School. In the building his steps echoed along the empty, dark hallways, and when he thought how many years he had spent in this school, and that his class was the last of a long, shadowy line to graduate from it, that it would soon be demolished, he felt quivery. He was finished with it, and it was finished. He saw a friend floating like a ghost at the far end of the hall and wanted to call out; the door closed and he was left in that early-morning gloom he had known so often in this building.

In his old classroom he got his report card and, almost running, emerged from the building into sunlight. The air was cool and moist, and he began to run across the hardened dirt of the playground. He felt a breathless excitement: he had finished something, was done with it, and now looked forward to new adventures.

At home he ate a quick breakfast, made sandwiches for lunch, and got his weapons; he carried a .22 Savage rifle and wore a .22 H&R pistol on a belt which also held a hunting knife and canteen. His mother wanted him to go with her to help finish decorating a Rose Festival float, but he had his own plans.

Today he would find Lost Lake.

By 9:30 he was crossing the empty fields of the neighborhood, the sun cutting through the high mist and lifting the dew from the weeds. Horace waited in his front yard, and together they walked across Foster Road and down 99th Street through Dwyer's mill. Johnson Creek was sluggish with mill refuse. A Hyster driver waved and yelled something; the saws whined and steam pumped from a dozen outlets drifted into the sky. Past the mill they walked in the shadow of logs stacked forty feet high.

Beyond the logs the road led them into the country.

To their right was Indian Rock, an old stone quarry, and then the road narrowed, turned, and they began their ascent up Mt. Scott. There were a few houses, but the land was undeveloped. On the corner, overlooking the mill, was a modest house, distinguished because it had the only swimming pool in Lents; it was Chris's impression that the owner had bought this piece of land because he could easily drain his pool down the hill. Farther on was Nigger Tom's shack, a dilapidated eyesore. There were only a few houses between, but these two showed the extremes: from what passed in Lents as affluence, to what was certainly poverty.

At the end of the road was Lincoln Memorial Cemetery.

They walked under the wrought-iron gates and began the steep climb, sometimes following the road, sometimes cutting across the graves. The oldest graves had tall stones and ornate Gothic lettering; they dated from the nineteenth century, and this concept of time and death made Chris's scalp crawl. Under the tall firs the stones were partly covered with a thick green moss. They climbed upward past newer graves, with flat stones, and got to the four silver World War I howitzers.

They were now high enough to see Portland. The eye followed the main streets, 82nd to Foster, Foster to Powell, westward to the river; downtown tall buildings shimmered in the sun. The *Journal* building with the clocks in its tower; the PGE building, Meier & Frank's, Lipman Wolfe, and above the city Council Crest and Skyline Drive.

They rested, then walked over the ridge and downhill toward the reservoir which marked the edge of the cemetery, and past it; entered the definite line of mature Douglas Fir which was the edge of the woods. Chris looked up before entering the trees, to see Mt. Scott rising steeply, the tops of its thick woods reflecting the sunlight.

Once inside that line of trees he felt changed, moved back in time; where there had been sunlight there was now darkness, where he and Horace had been exposed they were now hidden. They followed the familiar foot-trail through the trees, moving like Indians single-file, not speaking, the carpet of needles cushioning their steps. The woods were cool, dark, illuminated only where a thin sunshaft could filter through the high trees. He carried his rifle ready in the crook of his right arm, felt the weight of the pistol on his hip. In these woods he was not pioneer or cowboy or legionnaire, but all those and more as he padded through silent woods, armed, alert, content.

Usually they walked about a half-mile along this trail and then turned back, but today they followed it along a ridge and through a clearing. When it broke into the open they saw only blue sky; the firs cut off their view of the city, and they could well imagine it didn't exist. There were no houses on Mt. Scott, and they had never seen any people on the trails; the only things which moved in the dense woods were gray tree squirrels or birds.

Beyond the clearing the trail ended and they pushed through the dense undergrowth; they stumbled, cursed, held their rifles high so they wouldn't get scratched. They struggled uphill, stomping bushes back, sweat pouring through shirts until, about noon, quite by accident, they found Lost Lake.

They broke through the brush and saw dark water below them, a small, spring-fed lake tucked among the trees. Chris had been all over the mountain many times but he had seen the lake only once before, when Mal had shown it to him.

They ate lunch beside the lake. Peanut butter sandwiches, cookies, and an apple tasted great after the long, arduous climb. Chris drank from the canteen, the water metallic tasting and warm, and imagined himself hunting in the Rockies. Beside the small lake they talked about the movie, *Beau Geste,* which they had seen the week before at the new Century theater, and *Four Feathers,* which they hoped to see. They talked about going downtown on Saturday, and relived an especially harrowing descent they had once made on bikes down 112th Street hill. A breeze moved the trees' upper branches, and the heat sifted down; fir needles oozed a warm, rich odor. Chris lay back and looked straight up into the blue sky and wished that the world would never change.

Later they began to wander down the mountain. They found their familiar trail after an hour of struggling through brush, and were soon out of the trees. Now the route was unobstructed and it was all downhill. They walked past the reservoir, through the cemetery, past Indian Rock and Dwyer's mill.

They stopped to play in Johnson Creek and found a waterdog struggling along the bank; Horace grabbed it before it could get away. He said he was going to take it home but when they crossed the Galloping Goose tracks they heard the distant rumble of the trolley. Chris laid a penny and two nails on the tracks, and Horace, with a grin, tied the water dog in place with long strands of grass.

The steel tracks began to hum, and they saw the Galloping Goose, heard its mournful hoot as it approached Foster Road; it came toward them, the headlight like a single eye, the car swaying from side to side until it threatened to tip. They stood beside the tracks, fearless in the face of this danger, and as the trolley thundered past it blew its whistle to warn cars crossing 99th Street: the noise of whistle and steel wheels on tracks was terrific, and then it was past and in the ominous silence they looked down at their trophies.

Scotch Broom

During the night a heavy rain had fallen, and as he walked through the fields wet grass beat against his pant legs. The tall stalks bent with the weight of water, and spider webs were etched in bright patterns. Overhead the sky was blue, and as the sun broke from the low clouds in the east the field sparkled.

He had awakened early, a sense of excitement building. He had eaten breakfast quickly, and was out the door as his father left for work. He hurried across the fields toward Horace's house, wondering about the beautiful, nervous excitement that made him want to shout.

He began to run, shattering the delicacy of wet grass. As the sun rose a ground mist began to grow, rising to knee-level before it dissipated. There were four blocks of fields between his house and Horace's, and their growth ranged from grass to Scotch Broom and Oregon Grape to wild blackberries. As he crossed into the second he saw that the Scotch Broom had blossomed overnight, changing the field into a profusion of yellow. The bushes drooped with the weight of the rain but they were still over his head. Then he was standing within the bushes, the world shut off, the odor of alfalfa and sage overpowering, and he saw that each tiny yellow blossom was encased in a perfect drop of rain.

Smells

The cinnamon odor of lilac and roses drifting through the screen reminded him of Kool-Aid popsicles he had made in the refrigerator using toothpicks for sticks.

In the chicken house the smell of whitewash, Lysol, and chicken crap filled the darkness, and the thickness of straw forced itself into his nostrils.

On cold nights, while he listened to the radio in the front room, he enjoyed dropping fragments of airplane dope, dried like snot, on the oil heater. The tiny transparent trailing would curl, begin to smoke, and suddenly burst into flame. His own spit danced against the hot metal with a scorched smell.

He loved the smell of cordite, shell cases, gun oil; he would sniff the greenish brass shells of his .32 rimfire. He loved the smell of leather: his revolver holster and belt, the loops of bullets, the heavy sling of his rifle. A familiar odor was the metallic smell at the end of his B-B gun, where the blue metal became a copper-colored sunburst.

Old paper: the stale smell of his comic books and pulp magazines, like ear wax. The oily smell of old *National Geographics*. The books in the Lents library all smelled of institutional must, as if they were often damp. He found these odors, and their associations, pleasant.

The beautifully sharp odor of tobacco against his lips; the illicit taste of Loganberry wine and Olympia beer.

Some of the best times he associated with the strong, pitchy odor of fir trees: lying in a bed of brown needles on a hot day, the air charged with the pungent smell, or standing under a fir in the rain. Every field had a different smell, depending upon the weather and temperature. The smell of Oregon Grape in the fall, the seeds popping. The smells of rain: steamy on a hot sidewalk, green and pungent during the spring, constant during winter, the leaves wet and rotting underfoot like fish scales. On Halloween the masks got wet and sagged around the wearer's face, the fake hair a sodden mass, the overwhelming odor of cheesecloth.

The odor of dust cooking on the tubes of his radio late at night.

At the Branch

When he got to the corner he began to pedal faster and he swung into view pedals flashing, leaned the bike over, whipped it from the street around the corner and up onto the sidewalk and slid to a stop in the gravel beside the branch office. The five boys who sat in the shade on the east side looked up at his arrival, then continued to flick stones onto Foster Road in a bored, aimless manner. The door was still locked.

"Where's Allen?" Chris asked. Allen was the Branch Manager and it was his responsibility to get here early, to open the branch, and to distribute the papers.

"He quit," Billy said.

"No he didn't, he got fired," Cal said. He was Billy's brother, and fought with him as well as with everyone else. "He was letting the guys piss on that stove and the morning crew was raising hell."

Although it was summer, often someone would stuff the tin stove with the papers which were wrapped around the bundles and start a fire; when the stove's thin sheet metal began to glow red hot there was always someone who would urinate on it. The smell was bad enough at 5:00 p.m.; it was terrible twelve hours later when the morning crew arrived.

"He quit," Billy insisted. "He's going to start high school and he doesn't want a paper route anymore."

"You're out of your gourd, pud," Cal said, and slammed his fist into his brother's shoulder. They began to scuffle in the gravel and the others looked on with mild interest.

Chris sat in the shade and picked up a length of wire which had been used to bind a bundle of papers; he straightened it, found another wire, and tied the two together. He did this with six pieces, until he had made a single long wire, and when he had finished he walked to the edge of the sidewalk. Traffic was light on Foster Road, and when no cars were in sight he swung the long wire in an arc and let it fly into the air; it flashed, swinging, and dropped across both overhead trolleys for the electric bus. There was a bright flash and crackle. The wire rocked in the air, like a silver fish out of water. No matter how many times he had wired the trolleys he always felt the same intense excitement.

Allen still had not arrived when the beat-up yellow *Oregonian* panel arrived and the man threw the bundles of papers on the sidewalk and sped off. Two boys who were in a hurry to get going picked up bundles and took them into the shade where they struggled with the wire; the cutters were locked inside the branch, but after they bent the wire back and forth for several minutes a strand broke. They ripped out a handful of papers until there was enough slack to remove copies intact, and they began to roll them.

A bus came down Foster; the trolleys hit the wires, carried them along the cables and at every intersection of cross cables there was a flash and puff of smoke.

Chris had begun to pick up more pieces of wire when a black Chevrolet Fleetline pulled to the curb and Fowlwick got out. He was the Assistant District Manager and a senior in the high school where Chris would be going next fall. Fowlwick brushed back his sharp crew-cut, flipped his cigarette on the sidewalk and stepped on it without breaking stride, the toe of his gleaming oxblood-colored brogue mashing it into the cement. He wore spotless white cords and a Hawaiian shirt. Without a word he unlocked the door to the branch.

"Where's Allen?" Billy said. "He quit?"

"He got fired, right?" Cal said.

Fowlwick looked at them, and then smiled. "Let's just say that Allen is no longer associated with the company."

The air inside the building was roasting, and when Chris had got his papers for his two routes, 1551 and 1552, he went back outside to roll them. He was filling the handlebar bag when Fowlwick rapped on the window and motioned to him. He looked around to see if the gesture was meant for someone else, and then went inside wondering what the hell was up now.

Fowlwick leaned against a desk in the corner. "Chris, you know that Allen is no longer branch manager." He paused, reached into the pocket covered with a large palm tree, and drew out a pack of Luckies. He lit one while Chris watched, confused, knowing that Allen was gone but unsure why he was gone and what it had to do with him. "We're going to need a new man, and I've been watching you." He lit the cigarette and blew out smoke, his eyes narrowing as if he could see through Chris. "What do you think?"

"What do you mean?" Chris asked, understanding but not quite.

"How'd you like to be Manager? Pays $4.65 a month. There are some responsibilities; for example, you'd have to be here every day, arrive early to unlock the branch, check out the papers, and tidy up after the boys have left. It's a management job, and could lead to something better."

Chris knew he meant the job of Assistant District Manager, or even District Manager. "Sure, okay," he said, awed and excited by the prospect of earning money and of being chosen from all the other boys.

"Good," Fowlwick said, reaching to grasp Chris's hand while his other hand gripped Chris's shoulder, a movement which embarrassed Chris but which also made him feel like an adult. "I knew I could count on you. By the way, there's one other thing." Chris looked up as he sensed rather than heard the shift in tone. "You have to keep these guys from pissing on the stove. It smells terrible in here when the morning guys get here."

"I can do it," Chris said, sure that he could. With that extra money he could buy a Civil War sabre from Horace, or two Fiji throwing spears which were at Dicken's Curiosity Shop, or a .32 calibre Bulldog pistol from Robert Abels, or–no, he told himself, he needed the money to buy a pair of English Brogue shoes for high school.

"Good," Fowlwick said, looking around the small room.

"Hell, they don't even *need* a fire in the summer."

The Lents Gang

On the corner they waited, smoking, laughing, standing around. The Flynn, Boozer, Jergens, Teddy Gaff, Billy Walker, others he didn't know. The Flynn always wore a sailor's cap far back on his high black wave of hair. Boozer's arms were tattooed. They wore black puchuko pants, cigarette pack rolled in the tee-shirt sleeve, and either cycle boots or highly polished brogues. Sometimes a girl waited with them, lips pursed around a cigarette.

He saw them there late at night from the back seat of his parents' car. What they conveyed under the dim street light was a sense of terror, of death. How did they live, he wondered; what did they do when they left the intersection? Although they were only a couple of years older, he imagined them thriving in an adult world. Once he had seen Gaff kick the hell out of The Flynn, had seen the blood-stained sailor cap roll to the curb while that crazy Indian, son of a professional wrestler, Chief Iron Eagle, stood over him. He felt embarrassed when he and his parents left the Aero Theater and ate Coney islands in the greasy spoon across the street, because he knew the gang was watching him. Did his parents think he did things like that?

But it was worse when he went to the Aero alone, especially on a week night–a time when he liked the theater best. A block away he had to put his money in his shoe and walk carefully among the toughs, trying to look casual. Off the curb, across the street, on the curb, past them his eyes straight ahead, past the drug store his heart pounding–only 100 feet to the Aero's marquee, where he could step aside, fish the quarter from his shoe and enter the theater's warmth when he heard a voice: "Hay kid. Comere."

The Path

The wax-yellow headlights floated down the hill toward him, and he threw the apple without thinking. He was already pumping his bike against the incline when he heard the crash of glass, a tire skidding along the asphalt, and then he was off the tree-lined sidewalk, around the corner, pedaling, thinking shoot why'd I do that? Past the houses he turned down a rutted road, skidding on rocks, the paper bag bouncing against his handlebars, then onto a path which intersected the field. Under a tall fir he pulled up, breathing hard, listening.

Christ, he thought, wondering why he'd thrown the apple–he was always doing something without thinking. Like the fight with Bingham, or trouble with his teachers, or the time he gave Billy Walker the finger. These momentous incidents gave him a guilt he couldn't shake.

He saw the car, a Model A Ford coupe, growl along the dark street, one headlight fuzzy in the night. Stupid, Chris thought–if they saw a paperboy had thrown it they could get him easy. He had enough trouble worrying about the Lents Gang. The feeble light stopped, backed up, bounced down the rutted road in low gear. Chris felt terror, and squatted beside his bike to peer through the brush; the car got to Harold Street, turned right, and disappeared.

Chris stayed low, sighting down the path to where the old Lents school rose ghostly and square. His was the last class to graduate from it before they built the new one. It was a fire trap. Sometimes he and other boys had crossed Harold Street at recess to play in this field, along this path. A hermit had lived in the slanting house beyond it; they had stolen apples from his gnarled trees and when he had come to chase them they had thrown the apples at him.

That seemed long ago to Chris. More recently he had imagined meeting Arlene Harr or Lou Ann Beecher on the path, and wondered what he would do. Would Martin's formula work? Talk awhile, take the cigarette from the handlebar and light up, share it with her. Swear a little, and, an arm reaching to encircle her, begin to tell a dirty joke. And then? He sometimes kissed his arm, as if practicing for the real thing.

But then he thought of school, the talk, his friends teasing him, people looking at him. Even if Arlene or Lou Ann were to walk up the path right now he would remain immobile beside his bike.

After the Movie

He left the Aero feeling like Alan Ladd, walking close to the shadows, whistling. The excitement of the film moved him along the street as he watched for The Flynn, Billy Walker, Gaff, or others of the Lents' Gang. In front of the drug store he saw Margaret and he stopped, awkward in the light which fell from the window, trying to think of something to say.

"You seen Martin anywhere?" he asked. Once in shop class he had made an aluminum bracelet and had engraved his initials over Margaret's on the inside, even though she was really Martin's girl. He had never shown the bracelet to anyone.

"No," she said, chewing her gum and smiling.

As he stood on the corner with his hands in his pockets, unsure what to do, he saw his father's long black car nose across the intersection. His father looked straight ahead, his profile sharp against the other car lights, and he shifted slowly into second gear. Chris was uneasy, wondering whether he had been seen, and then his father moved past, as if in slow motion: the thin mustache, hat brim tilted across his forehead, the cigarette bobbing between his lips, the car moving past into the night.

Horace's Room

The difficult part was getting through the kitchen to the alcove. He stood at the door, apologetically removing one shoe and then the other, and crossed the spotless linoleum tiles. Everything in the house was immaculate, and Chris seemed to move in a cloud of dust. He got to the small room that Horace's father had carved from nothing, and began to climb the ladder; at the trapdoor he gave the secret knock.

"Who is it?" said the muffled voice.

"C'mon, let me in," Chris said, aware of Horace's mother somewhere around the corner.

"Your name," Horace said. "Speak, son of a camel."

"Hey, c'mon."

A bolt slid aside, and the trapdoor opened; once it closed Chris was in another world. The room was part of the attic, and finished entirely in knotty-pine; the wood glowed in the lamp light. It had short walls and a sharply pitched ceiling, which, Chris thought, was why Horace always walked bent over. The limited wall space was loaded with weaponry: two rifles, a pistol, a dueling foil, hunting knife, and two throwing spears. A large reproduction of a coat of arms was nailed over the desk, below a set of deer antlers. There was a bookcase, and on it a telescope. In some ways the room was like Chris', but, Chris thought, it was much more orderly and infinitely more mood-inspiring.

He walked to the open window and looked out at the huge fir trees that brushed the house. Through their branches he saw the moon, nearly full, in a cloudless sky. Chris had the feeling he was beyond time and space–he was part of the pyramids, the eternal sands of the desert, the crusades. There was another world that revolved around the daily routines of fathers, families, jobs; a world of adventure that orbited farther out, and to which only a few were admitted.

When he turned back to the room he felt as though he and Horace were conspirators of some sort, plotting history. Or sometimes, when they sat looking at their coin collections or were cleaning their guns, he imagined the room to be a hunting lodge such as he'd seen in magazines, the shadows flickering against the warm wooden walls.

"I wish we had some tobacco," Chris said.

"Hmmmmm," Horace said, shaking his head.

It wasn't that either was crazy about smoking, but rather that smoking fit in with the kind of life they imagined—drawing rooms with heavy leather chairs, the Explorer's Club, rum-soaked cheroots, massive pipes with silver lids, latticed windows, shutters, a fireplace, rows of books, crossed sabres on the wall, coin collections, a glass of brandy, a suit of armor, hunting dogs.

"Well," said Chris, leaning against the open window, looking at the moon which floated through eternity, "what'll we do?"

Modern Times

The Electric Eye

The store was a sweeping curve of glass, and all across the ceiling glowed blue-white fluorescent tubes. The doors opened as if by magic. At the entrance there were belt-high cement posts, and the boys discovered that each had a glass eye; these were aimed so that a constant light beam connected them. When you stepped inside the beam—or stood on the sidewalk, for hours, flashing your hand to break the beam's contact—the door opened.

The Perpetual Motion Donut Machine

It was a shabby building, with narrow board siding and a flat roof. Overhead was a wooden sign with a single bulb. Previously it had been a shoe repair shop, and the new owner hadn't even painted over the leather dying stains on the wall.

He had simply moved his massive aluminum and chrome donut making machine into the space by the front window, where the used shoes and boots had stood. The baker had to stand on a chair to pour batter into the top. Two nozzles ejected the perfect circles of batter into a tank of hot grease where they sizzled; paddles flipped them over. They floated brownly downstream toward a gate, where they fell, two at a time, on the cars. Each car was the size of a shoe sole, and the chain they rode on was endless; they cruised through the whole system, carrying the hot donuts out of the machine like a tiny railroad, toward the overpass which knocked them off where they lay in a pile. On the sidewalk people watched, hypnotized by the endless assembly line.

Horace

The summer breeze stirred the firs, and Chris, when he looked up from his *Bluebook,* was suddenly aware of the rich odor of warm pitch. From the ground's blanket of evergreen needles the odor continually emerged, like an endless spring. Chris loved the smell of the trees, the warmth which pressed from the ground, the golden dust motes which floated along the shadows.

Horace's mother brought them glasses of lemonade, and the drops of condensation ran down his fingers. In the hammock, where he was reading *True,* Horace laughed and said:

"Hitler's alive. In South America."

Horace was a taciturn boy who kept to himself. He was tall, fairly husky, but he walked with his head down and shoulders slumped forward in a way that suggested his body was folding in upon itself. His lips were perpetually shaped into a grin, as if he knew something very funny. The other kids called him the Professor, because he wore glasses and was always reading or was hunched over a sheet of paper, earnestly writing.

Chris was Horace's only friend.

Even Chris had ignored him until one day last year, when in art class he had walked past Horace's desk in the back row and had caught a glimpse of his work. It was a large sheet of paper filled with tiny figures—an army of men attacking a medieval castle. Chris had done drawings of battles in space or in World War II settings, but what differentiated Horace's drawing was the profusion of detail—every inch of the paper was filled with men shooting arrows, throwing spears and battleaxes, dumping boiling oil from ramparts; there were two catapults, a reserve of cavalry, flags, banners, drummers, buglers, tents. When Chris had asked what army was this, Horace had looked up, his eyes dreamy behind the thick glasses, and he had said that the Saracens were fighting the Infidels. Chris was amazed.

Over the next few weeks he got to know Horace better and they began to do the drawings together, each boy taking half of the sheet of paper. They roamed history, fighting with the French Foreign Legion, recreating Verdun, Anzio, Belleau Woods, the Crusades, the Khyber Pass. Chris learned about history, geography, warfare, weapons; when they weren't certain about the facts of a battle or a weapon they looked the subject up in the library. Their interests teetered between scholarship and frivolity, but for Chris the drawings were more educational than his classwork. Chris began to read what Horace read: Edgar Rice Burroughs, H.G. Wells, science fiction, pulps, *Beau Geste, The Stoger Arms Catalogue.* Together they rode the bus downtown every Saturday to visit the Oregon Historical Society to see the flintlock and cap-and ball firearms, to the museum to see a two-handed broadsword, to visit junk stores, second-hand stores, used book stores.

A whole new world opened for Chris. He still ran around with his old friends—Martin, Buzz, Mal, and the others, who were totally disinterested in Horace's interests—but he never tried to tell them what Horace was smiling about.

The Bird

The bird sat on the telephone wire along the street. He saw it as he went from the house to his room, but from this distance he couldn't tell whether it was a sparrow or a small robin. He thought what a shot that would make and aimed along his finger; the small target perched like a dark speck on his knuckle.

He went into his room and shut the door, debating what to do. From the weapons on his walls–knives and bayonets, a sabre, a shotgun, several rifles–he took down the .22 Savage, running his fingers over the walnut stock and the sleek, blued barrel. Opening the door a crack, he slid the muzzle out and slowly laid the gold front bead on the bird's silhouette. In his mind he heard the sharp report, imagined the neighbors running to the windows, saw the police car cruising past. He had shot the rifle from the house or yard several times–at distant arc lights, at birds–and each time he had been filled with fear and pleasure.

Taking a single cartridge from the bookshelf near the door, he slid it into the rifle's chamber and ran the bolt forward. He moved the gun until only its muzzle protruded from the door's slot; he took careful aim, and slowly squeezed the trigger. The flat crack exploded, bounced off the garage wall, and he quickly closed the door. He ejected the shell and put it into his pocket, ran an oiled patch through the rifle barrel, put the gun on the wall, and again opened the door.

The bird was gone.

With increasing trepidation he walked from his room around the house and stood on the front steps. He half expected to see some neighbors by their fences, talking and looking both ways to see what had happened, or a police car to cruise the road. His heart pounding at his temples, he made himself look along the pavement and there near the driveway, a small dull-grey fluff of evidence, was the bird, angled into the ground, tail in the air like a crashed plane.

Fantastic

The rocket perched on a tail of white flame. It was two spheres joined by a girder-work; the lower sphere had four stabilizing fins which were partly obscured by the smoke and dust kicked up by the rocket's engines. From portholes on the upper sphere faces looked out on the stark landscape. The horizon stretched on all sides, uninterrupted by trees or grass, broken only by sheer rock outcroppings; they glowed in the light reflected from the engines, an aluminum sheen which emphasized the sterile, vegetation less topography. In the distance was a dome-covered city whose buildings looked like Technicolor mushrooms. Between the city and the rocket was a BEM, three eyes protruding from the globular head, clawlike appendages at the end of the cables snapping the air.

He was moved more by the drawings than by the stories.

Lying in bed in the morning, enjoying the sharp, cool breeze that eased through the room, he would stare at the graphics–the muscular hero, the scantily-clad woman, the incredible monster– and wonder what world, past or future, they came from. *The Shadow Out of Time. The Master Mind of Mars.* Why, he wondered, did the hero need a two-handed broadsword when he had a ray-gun? Why did the women wear so few clothes, and those almost transparent? Were the monsters really dragons of the past, or genetic mutations of the future? The pulpy odor of musty newsprint overwhelmed him, and his mind raced across the spectrum of time, past the silver turrets and multi-colored domes, far past the point of willful suspension of disbelief.

The Cigarette

By the time he crossed Johnson Creek again the paper bag was almost empty. Stopping under the trees beside the bridge, he unhooked the wire from the handlebar end and slid off the grip. He leaned the bike to that side, and a cigarette fell from the handlebar. It was slightly moist and had a brown stain along the edge; he had started to smoke it three times before.

As the butt touched his lips he recognized the sharp, acrid taste of tobacco. He got a wooden watch from the pocket of his Ike jacket and after several tries with his thumbnail the match flared. In the pale of light he puffed gently, held the smoke, and slowly let it out. The taste was always new, a strange mixture of sensations which suggested travel, exotic places, tough guys.

Flipping the match into the creek he watched the slow current carry it away.

For a long minute he felt peacefully alone, floating on some solitary island. The idea of such solitude sent a chill up his back. Inhaling again, he was dizzy, and felt a sudden panic sweep his body–the tobacco, danger, the excited fear of being caught–and he again snubbed out the butt, put it inside his handlebar, replaced the grip, the wire hook, the paperbag, and pedaled away, his head reeling with the first stars of the evening.

The Lost Patrol

They came down from the second balcony, down the wide, carpeted stairs into the odor of popcorn. He felt a sense of excitement and mystery in this theater with its carvings of elephants and tigers, and the dome which had a sky-scene more real than the sky itself, He moved with the motions of the film, acting it out: *I say there chaps* the pilot had said, stepping from his biplane to be hit by the unseen sniper's bullet. One by one they were picked off, and you never saw the enemy until the very end; it was scary and mysterious, and it conveyed exactly what he imagined desert fighting was like. At least what it was like in those days of World War I.

In the lobby his father stopped to roll a cigarette; he lit it at the front door, the smoke curling into the busy street. When they had gone in it had been daytime; now it was night. He had mixed emotions about going to the show with his father: he wanted someone to talk with, to re-enact the movie with, to goof off with, but on the other hand he liked walking up the dark street toward the car, just the two of them far from home.

"I like when the guy climbs up the palm tree and they ask what he sees; 'I see something. I see a rifle barrel' and then he comes pitching out."

"Me too," his father said. "Reminds me of *All Quiet on the Western Front.* I liked that one too." He started laughing, almost choking on his smoke. "They were in the trenches and everyone was to keep real quiet. Then as they crawled under the bob wire one guy farted!"

He laughed again, and Chris laughed, uneasily, slightly embarrassed; he looked behind them on the dark, empty street to see whether anyone else had heard.

Lents: Early Sunday Morning

The sun angled across the grey sidewalk and black asphalt; shadows were cool, plum-grey. The flat brilliant light emphasized textures: stucco and terra-cotta, tiled facades and angled drain pipes, bricks beneath concrete, the sidewalk's age, garbage cans, the streets like vacant fields, the empty mouth of an alley.

No building was taller than a telephone pole: Rexall and Mt. Scott drugs, Stella's variety, Menashe's, Butterfield's grocery, Eggiman's meat market, Harold's cafe. All had their awnings drawn; the endless spiral of Bud's barber pole was still. Missing letters on the Aero's marquee, and inside the litter, the cold popcorn, the urinal's trickle. The fire hydrant's shadow was a long dog. Near the curb a newspaper threatened to move.

Second story rooms sent messages with the semaphore of shades. Here was the mystery: who would live over Reilly's tavern, the Rose Lantern, where the echoes of juke boxes and laughter were like fallen bones? Sauerkraut and sausage, tobacco smoke, stale beer, dustballs, wooden matches wedged in floor cracks. Like the Goodwill and secondhand stores these rooms displayed the dumb evidence of other lives. In time slippers would shuffle down dark hallways toward the bathroom, the coffee would perk, radio play Baptist music–a wracking cough, pipes rattling in walls, silverware clattering in the afternoons of memory. A faded wash dress would dance on the line between two chimneys, celebrating life.

But now the air was cool, brittle, slightly metallic, like stone or spice, and all defined with the clarity of a dream: this space, that structure, this place. The air continued upward. The sky was blue, unbroken by clouds, birds, smoke. One star was still visible directly overhead, growing dim.

Church

Because the air had a slight chill, like a knife blade held against the cheek, a last reminder of winter, he wore his suit to church. It was a beautiful grey sharkskin double-breasted suit, with padded shoulders and wide lapels. His mother thought he looked so nice in the suit, with a white shirt and his father's necktie, that almost every time he wore it to church she wanted to take his photograph.

He attended church irregularly, and, because his mother believed in the respectability she associated with church-going but was herself unable to settle on any one religion, he attended them all in a haphazard fashion: the Lutheran, the Four Square, the Baptist, the Methodist, and off and on over the years the Lents' United Brethren Evangelical Church. The only one he had never attended was St. Peter's where, his mother said, they drank wine.

He attended church without any particular enthusiasm, except for two things: he loved to walk to church on Easter when the season was changing and flowers sprang mysteriously from the grimy earth of winter–that was the only time when going to church made sense, as if the landscape reflected the sermon–he liked to wear his suit. When he put it on he felt as though he was a different person, as if he were in a movie. Sometimes when his parents were gone he would put it on and walk around the room admiring himself in the mirror.

There was another reason for wearing the suit: it was the only time he could carry a concealed weapon.

As on this morning when, after his mother had checked him over, he went back into his room and took off the jacket. He fitted two loops of rawhide around his shoulders and attached them to his holster. He slid the loops around him until the holster hung under his armpit and he tied them.

The pistol was an H&R Model 922 with a six inch barrel; he checked the cylinder, saw that it was unloaded, closed and spun it, and placed the revolver into the open holster. Then he put on his suit jacket. The reflection in the mirror revealed no odd bulges; even when he stood straight, shoulders thrown back, the jacket did not appear unusual. He saw the broad expanse of grey cloth, the wide lapels, the ornate necktie, the sweep of hair which rode over his ears and the big wave in front cresting above his forehead.

He went into the house and started through it, but in the kitchen his mother jumped up from the table. "Hold it, kiddo," she said. She ripped a page from the Sunday paper, rubbed it against the plate of white margarine, and began to polish his dull, beat-up shoes.

"Aw, c'mon," he said, shuffling his other foot, growing impatient and slightly angry as she rubbed the margarine into every crack of the leather; under his armpit the five pound revolver began to slip downward.

She stood, and with her clean hand she began to tug at the suit, pulling the fabric, straightening the lapels, leveling the tie's knot. He was afraid she'd feel the pistol butt under his shoulder.

"Stand straight!" she said, pushing at his kidneys. "Fish, I think it's those rubber bands that make you walk so stooped." The latest fad was to attach a rubber band from the top button of one's pants to the lower button of the shirt; it gathered the material together for a flat front and a bloused back.

"Gotta go," he said, pulling away and walking through the front room to the porch. Outside, he sniffed the cool morning air: roses and lilac blossoms, a trace of dew, the Japanese plum tree in flower. Low clouds drifted across the face of Mt. Scott, and he wished that he were on the mountain.

His sister came out, wearing the new pink dress their mother had made, black patent leather shoes, her hair tied with a pink ribbon, and carrying the family Bible. They walked along the street toward Ramona, the only side street in Lents with a sidewalk. Chris loved these summer mornings which had the coolness of spring: daffodils and gladioli bloomed, apple and cherry trees were in blossom, the air had a freshness which seemed almost visible.

They had gone about a block when the pistol began to feel awfully heavy, and as they walked he had to keep pushing it up.

"What's the matter?" his sister asked.

"Nothing," he said.

"Why do you keep scratching?"

"None of your beeswax," he said, trying to walk with his shoulders thrown back with the hope that the gun would stay in place.

Lents was almost empty, and not until they approached the Evangelical United Brethren Church did they see other people. A group had gathered at the front door, to shake hands; kids played tag on the sidewalk. He and his sister pushed past them and entered the building.

At this point he always felt odd. No matter that he had done this many times, he always felt awkward and unsure of his movements and was conscious that he was being watched. They walked jerkily past the rear pews, which were mostly occupied by old men, and found seats near the center.

As his sister looked around for a friendly face, Chris slid his hand inside his coat and shifted the pistol into place. Then he relaxed, looked up at the high ceiling and the tall, but gaudy, stained-glass windows.

Soon the preacher entered from behind the choir and Mrs. Canary, the organist, played a few bars. "Let us sing hymn number seventy-two," he said, arms outstretched. Chris reached for the hymnal and felt the pistol's weight slide forward. He pushed it back, thumbed through the hymnal until he found the right page and began to sing "Building on the Rock." Beside him the voice of his sister was small but loud.

The preacher opened his sermon, and as it grew in pitch and intensity it was punctuated by cries of "Amen" from the back rows. Every time someone called out Chris felt personally embarrassed. But, then, he thought that most of the people here were pretty strange, and about half of them seemed related: they had long, sharp noses, receding chins, lantern jaws, and prominent Adam's apples. Poor dumb Okies, his mother called them. Several of the women wore incredibly thick glasses, which gave them an appearance of hope mixed with despair.

There were others, a mixture of kinds, but what they had in common was that they seemed to live lives which bore no resemblance to his own. There were stocky young men with pink cheeks and curly hair who, Chris imagined, worked all week and played sandlot baseball on the weekend; they probably rode delivery bicycles, worked as apprentice carpenters or stock-boys. There were broad-faced young women without a trace of makeup; skinny girls with thick glasses and flowered dresses. Their Sunday school teacher had a crew-cut, a letter-man's sweater, and was always incredibly cheerful, as if the letter had been awarded for optimism; he reminded Chris of a perpetual Boy Scout. Chris thought it was strange that he hardly ever saw these people, or people like them, outside of church—where did their lives take them the rest of the week?

When the sermon ended they sang another song, and then the congregation broke up for separate activities. His sister went downstairs for her Sunday school class. Chris waited in the alcove beside the front door until she had disappeared, and then he slipped out the door, went down the steps and walked briskly toward Lents.

The sun warmed the expanse of cloth at his back and he began to relax. He loved the morning air, the street, sun, and the emptiness of Lents on a Sunday. Light fell in strong angles across the buildings. Wood smoke rose from a chimney into the pure blue sky. The air had a thin, exciting odor. Chris felt happy to be alive.

At Woodstock Street he slowed, studied the pile of junk in the window of the second-hand store, and crossed the street to study the Goodwill's junk. Then he crossed back to study the Aero's marquee and posters. *Joan of the Ozarks* and *Along the Old Spanish Trail.* He hoped to see them.

He walked on the shady side of the street to the corner and stood in front of Mt. Scott Drug Store, the only business that was open. He looked at his reflection in the window—the wide shoulders, the sculpted hair-do which rose wave upon wave and came to a DA in the back, the draped cloth, the greasy shoes—and after hoisting the gun's weight he entered the store like an

30

adult. For a split-second, as the door hung open, he thought how easy it would be to rob the store; there were only two customers at the counter, and the woman behind it. But he continued walking toward the rear of the store where the comic books were racked. He read a dozen comics in a half-hour–*Boy, Detective, Jungle, Real Clue, Crime Does Not Pay* (hoisting the gun under his arm)–and as the pharmacist had not yet arrived there were no interruptions.

When he left he hurried back to the church; this was the awkward moment. He always felt slightly guilty when he had skipped Sunday school, and he had to merge with the others outside the church and pretend that he had been there for some time. It was like walking backwards into a building to give the illusion of leaving.

On the sidewalk he could hear the faint strains of the littlest kids singing "Jesus Loves Me" and he knew that he was early. He crossed the street to take another look at the Eggiman boy's 1936 Ford 5-window coupe; it was solid black, with skirts, dual pipes, echo cans, lowered rear end, Hollywood hubcaps, and leopard skin interior. As Chris stood beside it, smelling the sun which baked off the black paint, he longed for something like this.

He looked up as the people poured from the church, and he saw his sister in the crowd; he crossed the street again, and together they walked home, kicking rocks, looking in windows, talking. The pistol had grown to be an intolerable weight by now, and he longed to get home, get the gun and suit off, and climb into some comfortable old clothes.

When they got to the final corner they saw their mother in the yard watering bushes; when she saw them she dropped the hose and ran into the house, emerging moments later with the camera in hand. The sun was out, the suit was like a tent holding in heat, and Chris was sweating; he was in no mood to have his photo taken. He tried to get out of it, but she made them line up beside a big rose bush while she squinted into the viewer. "Smile now, come on." He tried to smile until she snapped the picture: they were frozen in time, grinning, the Sunday clothes, the incredible suit, his hair slicked into a series of waves, and–he imagined later, whenever he would see the photo in the family album—under his armpit, against the expanse of grey sharkskin material, the hint of a pistol grip.

Eating Out, Part I

Under the elm the shade was cool, and he watched the drops trickle slowly along the dark glass bottle of his father's Oly, saw the small bubbles rise in a continuous stream from the bottom.

His contentment was intense. He listened: the rhythm of a lawnmower being pushed in steady strokes, a dog barking, neighbors talking over a fence, birds, the sounds he would hope for on a summer Sunday afternoon. He loved the heavy, exotic odor of cut grass, hollyhock, roses, glads, fir trees. Like a wave one level below these came the odor of cooked meat, and it pleased him.

The Sunday *Oregonian* had been delivered the evening before, and today he was free of that. After supper he could lie in the hammock or ride his bike around the neighborhood or listen to the radio; later he could sit in the warm air and watch the stars emerge one by one. The sense of freedom and excited contentment clawed at his spine like small fingers.

His sister brought plates and silverware. His mother came out with glasses and a pitcher of sparkling red Kool-Aid. He poured himself a glass, and his fingers trembled with excitement against the cold surface.

His mother returned, carrying a large brown bowl of potato salad and a pan of fried chicken. When the lids were removed the smell of food mingled with the odor of cut grass, flowers, fir, almost overpowering him. He got a drumstick and felt the delicious meat come clean from the bone.

Eating Out, Part II

"How long've they had drive-ins?" Chris sprawled on the back seat reading the neon script: Merhar's Drive-Inn. Rust streaked the white brick wall, a window was broken, the pavement was littered with wrappers, straws, napkins; his mother kept wishing that they would clean the place up. Chris loved to come here, because Merhar's had things you couldn't get anywhere else, like root-beer or banana milkshakes, and Coney Islands with chopped onions and hot sauce.

"Never saw one before, oh, say, five or six years ago," his father said.

How strange to eat in the car! Sometimes they came here after a Sunday drive, or when they worked on the house, or if their small kitchen was too hot. When the food came the car's interior filled with the odor of steamed bun and wiener longer than any he had ever seen, chili sauce and onions, French fried potatoes, root beer milkshakes. He loved it!

Heat waves danced on the asphalt. 82nd Avenue on a Sunday afternoon was nearly empty. Above them the sky was a perfect blue bowl unsullied by even the tiniest cloud. Suddenly, for a split-second he had a vision of himself as a child at this intersection: hot mohair upholstery, the brilliant glint of chrome, motion, a new cap gun, the taste of Nehi strawberry pop, a cloudless sky and in it an airplane spelling out in smoke the words Pepsi Cola. What did it mean? he wondered. Was it one day (the Fourth of July?) or a bunch of days mixed into one?

"Here we go," his father said as the car-hop fastened the tray to the window. He began handing out food, the hot Coney Island, the cold glass of milkshake. "Don't spill back there."

"She sure has got tight slacks," his mother said of the carhop. "Fish, I wouldn't go around like that."

"She sure has," his father agreed.

Chris bit into the Coney Island, sniffed the exotic hot sauce and chopped onion, and chewed with slow delight. Heat began to build inside, and he sipped the banana shake.

A car pulled in next to them. It was a black convertible with two couples; the men had high waves in their hair, and the women wore bandanas. The driver leaned his back against the door and flipped cigarette ashes over his head; he laughed loudly at something. One woman laughed while the other drank from a beer bottle. In the front seat of their car his mother was trying to see the people without being seen. "Ugh, fish," she said, grimacing.

One thing Chris liked about Merhar's was the kind of people who hung around it. He always saw wild-looking people here, like the men who sat on the fancy Harley-Davidsons parked near the kitchen door. They wore leather jackets with numerous chrome studs and stars; the cycles had saddle-bags, lights, reflectors, and fox-tails hanging from the handlebars.

Chris tried to imagine what their lives were like, and he decided that in some strange way they existed by continually facing death and eating the exotic food of Merhar's. They were greasy, wild, noisy, and rode or drove noisy, wild machines which would be their death someday. It seemed a strange, but not unpleasant, way to live and die.

The door of the black convertible opened and a woman got out and walked toward the building. She wasn't much older than he was, Chris decided, and yet in her white blouse and Levis she looked like a Petty girl drawing. He could not imagine what her life was like. As she walked past the cycle riders, they yelled something at her; she gave them the finger and went inside. Chris concentrated on his food.

Cigars

"Uhhhh," Horace said for the ninth time, his glasses clouded, his lips pulled back into his idea of a pleasant smile, "excuse me. Buy some cigars .... "

The man pushed past without speaking, and Horace turned to the stairwell where Chris waited; he grinned and shrugged his shoulders. And why shouldn't the man push past? —who'd want to buy cigars for two kids standing in the shadows beside the basement stairs in Meier and Franks, looking like awkward Amboy Dukes?

An old lady apparently would, and she came toward Horace as if she knew what he wanted. Chris saw her nod twice, take the money, and go to the tobacco section where unwrapped cigars were on sale two for five cents. Chris shook his head in astonishment, and wondered whether she was a store detective. She returned, handed the bag to Horace with a smile, and Chris saw Horace mumble a thanks.

He slouched forward and came to where Chris waited, moved past, and then they were running up the stairs two at a time, laughing. The toilets on the lower floors were full, but by the fourth floor they were pretty empty, and at the sixth there was only one guy. Chris and Horace leaned against the wall while the man washed his hands and dried on the endless towel; they gasped, trying to catch their breath, laughing with excitement between gasps, and as the man opened the door to leave he stopped to look at them in an odd, scrutinizing way.

When they were alone they went into the cubicle near the wall and latched the door. Horace pulled two cigars from the sack and handed one to Chris, who stroked the tightly packed tobacco with trembling fingers, and breathed deeply of the sharp greenish odor. The cigar was solid, streamlined, and beautifully real; as he held it he thought of baronial halls, fireplaces, latticed windows.

"Light me up, will you, old man?" Chris asked. Horace held the match to him, touched the cigar, which began to glow and then flame. The smoke came through fine and clear, just like he'd seen it happen in movies; he blew out a steady stream. "Darn good draw," he said.

Horace lit his, chuckled, sucked his cheeks in and then let the smoke emerge in a stream; he held the cigar at arm's length to study it. "Hmmmmmm," he said.

Chris sucked in another mouthful of smoke, let it out slowly, and tapped the ash into the toilet bowl. He felt a vague sensation, not unpleasant, like a hand reaching around the back of his head. His tongue touched the film that had built up on his teeth, tasted the sourness that swam in his mouth. But he certainly wouldn't quit until Horace did.

They had just taken a series of quick puffs and were studying the ends of the cigars when they heard the whoosh of the outer door opening, heard voices talking business. There was a short silence, the running of water. Then one voice said, "Damn, it's sure smoky."

Horace and Chris bent over, holding their sides, trying to stifle laughter. They imagined the businessmen walking into the smoke-filled room, wading through clouds in their neat suits. "Must be on fire," one said, running water. Chris held his sides, suppressed laughter forcing the breath from his lungs; he wondered if the men were serious or were kidding.

Then it was quiet, and they wiped the tears from their eyes.

They tried to puff on the cigars but every time their lips formed around the cigar laughter interfered. " 'Must be on fire' he said," Chris said, giggling.

A fist pounded on the metal door and the noise echoed.

"C'mon out of there," a voice said.

They looked at each other in surprise, began to laugh, and Horace said, "Okay, be out in a minute."

"What're you doing in there?"

They dropped the cigars in the toilet, flushed it; Horace slid back the bolt and they walked out, arms gripping their packages.

The man was a custodian; he held the door open, and waved the clouds of smoke away as he looked inside the cubicle. He seemed to expect others to come walking out, like the carnival trick where a lot of clowns emerge from a tiny car. He glared at them, as if memorizing their faces. "What're you doing in there?" he said. "Don't you know there's a law against two people in one stall?"

The Buick Hood Ornament

"Go ahead," Martin said. "I dare you."

"Dares go first," Chris said, already flinching as Martin's fist smashed into his shoulder.

"Don't give me that dares-go-first crap, boah. Let's see you shag-ass down there," Martin said, snuffling, cocking his head back, playing tough for the others.

Chris felt dismayed, because he had said he'd cop the Buick hood ring and now all the others were watching. Mal,

Verlyn, Harlan silently egged him on by their presence. He wondered how the hell he got into these situations.

"Move it, mutha. Unless you're chicken."

Chris turned and walked slowly down the sidewalk, past the old Rexall, past Reilly's tavern, past Menashe's fruit stand, to where the new Buick was parked. It was a black fastback sedan with bright white-walls, and at the top of the wide hood was the shiny rocket through the ring. All he had to do was step off the curb, grab the ring, twist, and run like hell. He sauntered beside the car's door, smelled its newness, and stood there, looking back at the corner where the others stood. Then he took a deep breath, and walked on past, hands in his pockets.

Waterdogs

Chris lay on the ridge and looked behind, down the tiered tombstones of the cemetery, past the twin WW I howitzers silver in the sun. Far beyond, Portland unfolded street by street toward the river and the downtown buildings which blazed like sheets of glass.

He loaded five shells into the clip of the Savage and before shoving it all the way in he slid a sixth into the breech, slamming the bolt forward. He elevated the rear sight, rested the gun on the tombstone, and aimed at the reservoir which nestled in a pocket of the cemetery. He waited. Soon a patch of brown floated to the surface and broke water, the legs moving like antennae. It was a difficult downhill shot and Chris placed the gold bead over the waterdog, lowering it until it was deep in the veed rear sight. He took a long breath, squeezed the trigger. The shot cracked and a geyser of water sprang six inches from the waterdog, which rolled over to show a stomach that was brilliant orange in the sunlight.

Coin Collecting

He turned on the radio and sat before it, the money spread over the rug. Opening the copy of the paper he had brought home, he found the radio schedule and carefully circled the evening's programs:

7:00	Sands Time			
7:15	Sands Time			
7:30			Dist. Attorney	
7:45			Dist. Attorney	
8:00		Jack Kirkwood		
8:15		Perry Como		
8:30	Lux Theater			
8:45	Lux Theater			
9:00	The Norths			
9:15	The Norths			
9:30				Hit Parade
9:45				Hit Parade
10:00			I Love Mystery	

The dial was small, round, and yellowed with age. The voices seemed to come from far away, and sometimes he imagined he had tuned in programs broadcast years before he was born–strange voices that strained to be heard, the product of some electronic experiment lost in the sound waves.

When he was sick he listened to the soap operas–Just Plain Bill, One Man's Family, Helen Trent. Fever pressed like the weight of old newspapers, his eyes burned against the room's darkness, and he wondered where these people lived, what they did. They did not seem like anyone he knew.

Now, while he listened, he counted his paper route money, wrapping the bills with a rubber band. He sorted the coins into piles, and found four Indian Head pennies, a dozen Buffalo nickels, and two Barber dimes. His best find was a 1914 Barber half-dollar and a 1912 Liberty Head nickel, the latter worn almost as smooth as a slug. The coins he needed he pressed into his albums and the others he put into a small leather pouch his grandmother had given him.

The coins had a tactile quality, and he liked their weight.

They were real, and when he looked at them he had a sense of time, of other eras, and imagined the coins moving from hand to hand over all the years.

The Battle

They waited beside the fence, peering into the growing dusk for the slightest movement. In pockets and the cradle of their arms they carried all the green apples they could hold; the enemy was the Sanford brothers and Ronnie Dart, and they lobbed apples at them every evening just for the sheer joy of being pursued.

Horace chuckled, and hurled an apple far into the pasture, but there was no response; the enemy had gone in for the night. Somewhere along the fence a cricket began to chirp, a piercing sound of steel being scratched; the fields reverberated with sound, and overhead came the *cur-loo* of a night bird.

"Die, son of a camel!" Horace threw an apple at a telephone pole, and it hit with a solid thunk. Chris charged, throwing three fast ones with unerring accuracy; the salvo echoed into the darkness.

They waited in silence, balancing an armful of apples.

Then on impulse Chris turned, his arm raised, and cried, "Kill for Kali!" He threw, saw Horace duck, laugh, and out of the darkness an apple swished past his head.

"In the name of Allah," Horace shouted, firing, running for the grove of fir trees.

Chris ducked, and fired into the trees until he had only two apples left. He ran toward the fence, keeping low, and he waited for any movement. The moon broke suddenly from the clouds, washing the fields, the rutted road, the grove of firs in a silver light. Behind him, he knew, the PGE sign would silhouette his position, and so he kept low until he saw a flash of movement in the trees.

"Unclean! Low born!" He sprang from the tall grass, firing quickly with both apples and his reward was the cry of pain that rose on the night air like a voice from a minaret.

39

Sleeping Out

Their tent was a sheet thrown over the clothesline wire and tied to pegs in the ground. Martin used the wire as an antennae for the crystal radio; they each had an earphone, but Martin controlled the key.

The Hit Parade program ended and the news came on: *up the famous marble staircase to Fahey-Brockman's—names make news and so do these.*

The stars spread beyond the trees in a cloudless sky, and Chris recalled a film where stairs grew from the stage to tower over buildings, rising to the stars; a celestial music accompanied those who climbed this bridge between heaven and earth. The stairs, in his mind, symbolized infinity.

In his sleeping bag he felt contentment. He thought about the stars, and the sounds that carried over the air waves. He was puzzled but excited by the mysteries of space and eternity, and comforted by the music that came from somewhere to touch him.

Work

His mother could have just let the water run from the machine through a hose to the ground near the back steps, but she thought that that would wash away the house's foundation and so he had to *carry* the water in a big pot to more distant places.

The back porch smelled of wet newspapers and wet wood.

He crawled under the machine to open the drain; gray water fell into the familiar aluminum pot, a thin layer of gray soap frothing up. He leaned against a cardboard box filled with old canning jars and newspapers; with the wet heat of washday the back porch was like a steamy jungle. The machine was an agitator type with gray rollers on the wringer, and he thought if they had a new automatic washing machine like Buzz's mother had he wouldn't have to empty it by hand. She even had a mangle.

He looked up at the open window of the porch and saw their willow, the neighbor's tall spruce, and a cloudless blue sky. A small breeze came through the screen door and went out the window; he could see it move the tops of the trees. He hated the work of emptying the wash water, but he loved days like this, the warm winds and cool shadows, the hot tar on the road, the heat waves shimmering along Foster Road and the brilliant light reflecting from store windows.

When the pot was full he shut off the drain and carefully carried the pot of water outside and down the steps. He walked from the shadow of the house into the front yard where the sun blazed. Tipping the pot he poured equal amounts of water over the small laurel, the box trees, the rose bushes–it killed aphids, his mother had said.

At least fifteen more trips would be required to drain the machine, and so he stood in the front yard killing time. The grass was dark green and neatly trimmed; across the front a row of rose bushes bloomed bright red, pink, yellow, and, his favorite, salmon. Beyond was an apron of grass and the road, whose pavement ended after the next house. He looked across the open fields, where tall grass waved in the summer breeze. There were houses scattered among the outstanding fir and spruce trees, and to the south, a backdrop, Mt. Scott.

He savored the sunlight and shadow, the breeze which alternated warm and cool, the odor of flowers, cut grass, trees, fried meat. Already someone was cooking dinner. He loved the textures of summer, and things peculiar to summer–watermelon pickles, dark olives, potato salad, cold ham, lemonade–or was it because it *was* summer that he loved them?

He heard a car turn the corner and saw his father's long black Lincoln. As it slowed for their driveway, his father's face dust-covered and smiling framed within the open window, he remembered how when he was little he would run out to meet his father at the corner and ride the block home standing on the runningboard; when they had pulled into the driveway, a thin cloud of dust falling around them, the hot smell of car paint and upholstery swelling into the yard, his father would give Chris his lunchbox which usually contained a cookie or a half sandwich, the air within the box smelling strongly of salami, hot mayonnaise, and wilted lettuce. He'd thought the remnants a treat. That was when he had been a little kid; he couldn't imagine eating something like that now.

Modern Times II

Dry Ice

"What's so cold it *burns?*" his father said, plunking the package of Fred Meyer ice cream on the kitchen table.

"Dry ice!" Chris said, thinking even as he said the words they seemed contradictory–how could ice be dry? And be so cold it would burn? His father tore off the wrapper and there among the folded newspapers were the chunks of ice. They smoked as if burning into the paper. Chris tried to pick up a piece but the pain was terrible; small yellow marks showed where the ice had burned his skin. He got a spoon and dropped the chunk into the sink, where it bubbled in a bit of water. Knowing that it was poisonous, he kept it away from the dishes and put it into a canning jar with some water. A row of bubbles trailed upward; each bubble formed on the surface like a smoky eye or cataract, then burst with a cloud of smoke. What he really wanted to do, every time they got some ice cream, was to pack all the chunks of dry ice in a jar with some water, screw the lid on tight, and run like hell. He imagined the pressure growing until the jar would explode in a cloud of white smoke, like a geyser of CO_2.

The X-Ray Machine

In Teeny's Shoe Store the machine was at the rear, and every time he went into the store he got his feet X-rayed. He stuck his feet in the hollowed space and looked through the viewer, as if he were watching a movie at the penny arcade. His skin dissolved, his bones were shadows, his self became visible. He moved a toe, saw the shadow respond like a lightning rod in a storm.

Fan Letter

Dear Dave,

I listen to you every night on your program and also on
Bunkhouse Jamboree. I write down all the songs that you sing
and I have made a folio of them. I like cowboy and hillbilly
music better than any other kind. I play the electric guitar and
hiawian. I am going to take my hiwian guitar and change it
into a spanish until I can buy a spanish. I have been down to
see your show a couple of times; I have met Dallas Turner and
Gene Evans in person.

Besides cowboy songs I also collect their autographs and
pictures.

The song I want you to play is Gene Autrys "Silver Haired
Daddy of Mine."

Your admirer and freind

When I grow up I want to have a show like Red Folley's. I
think your show is wonderful, but I like the way he has his
arranged, but I think they should take out Minnie Pearl or else
have her play something.

Shoeshine Bar

"Ever get any of that candy in?" Buzz asked. When he tried to
keep a serious expression on his face his mouth curved into a
smirk. Chris leaned on the counter, the back of the cash register's
ornate relief cool against his cheek. Above them a blow-fly
buzzed heavily in the heat, narrowly missing the orange fly-paper
which hung from the light.
    "What candy's that?" Mr. Orlando asked, wiping the white
enamel scale with a feather duster. The store was just a room,

the front of a house; he and his family lived in the rooms in back, and the building was the only business on a street lined with houses. He was a big man, always threatening to run out of breath, and yet he worked steadily and with great patience.

"You know, Shoeshine Bars," Buzz said, biting his lower lip in an attempt to maintain a serious expression. Buzz had made up the name of the imaginary candy bar, but if Mr. Orlando knew this he never mentioned it.

"Noooooo," Mr. Orlando said, bending to survey the rows of penny candy and gum and chocolate bars. "Noooo, I don't see any," he said. "I'll ask the driver on Wednesday."

"Okay, Virgil, good enough," Buzz said, laughing. Chris followed him to the pop machine, and he forced himself to laugh at their little joke. There was no such candy bar. Every time they came into the store Buzz pulled the same stunt; it had once really been funny, but lately it seemed less funny.

Bottles bobbed in the slightly chilled water. Buzz took a Royal Crown and Chris a Dad's root beer. "Put these on the account, Virgil," Buzz said. "We'll drink them here."

When they moved through the swinging doors they were hit by a blast of hot air; a breeze stirred the dust in front of the store, moving it down the street. They used the opener nailed to the wall, and sat on the board porch. Chris took a long drink of Dad's, a new brand, which lacked the sharpness of Hire's.

Harold Street lay flat and hot and shimmering, and empty of traffic; there weren't even any cars parked along the edges. In the afternoon heat the yards were empty. He couldn't hear any sounds of activity, except for the sharp clacking of a dust-colored grasshopper. The neighborhood had a peacefulness and serenity that made him feel affectionate for the streets without sidewalks, the dusty side-roads, the tree filled yards. Sometimes he imagined that he could see into the houses, into the lives, even though many of the people in the area were strangers to him.

Buzz's house was on the corner, tall and white, overshadowed by the huge English walnut tree. Chris thought it looked like a house in a movie, and he liked to walk through it. Some of the houses were fairly nice, but none were elegant; some were pretty run-down. He had decided that his own house was in-between, livable but lacking any character.

Buzz put his thumb on the lip of his bottle and shook it, releasing a stream of RC into the air. "Oh gawd," he said, laughing, watching Chris to see how he would react. Chris smiled, but thought it was a waste of money. Buzz always had money and his mother let him use her account at the store. That, he guessed, was the main reason why he went places with Buzz. Once Buzz's silly antics had attracted Chris, but sometimes they now made him feel uneasy.

Far down Harold a car slowly approached and as Chris watched it became a tall sedan; Mrs. Quorba, an angular, bird-like woman, gripped the wheel tightly as she crept past. "Hiya honey," Buzz yelled, waving, running to the edge of the road. He and Buzz had been friends for years, but in the past year he had not seen him often. Now he thought of how different his friends were–Buzz, Horace, Martin, Mal–and how he behaved differently with each of them. He could not imagine talking with Buzz about Lawrence of Arabia, nor could he imagine being with Horace and yelling at old women. He felt that his world was slowly changing, that he was changing.

Buzz stood beside the empty road chanting in a loud voice:

"Rattle up a snake's ass,
Paul shot a goose;
 Shot him in the asshole
And knocked his feathers loose."

Paul was Buzz's father. Chris smiled, and took a long drink of Dad's.

Alone

Heat baked down from the rafters, smelling of cedar shakes, pine boards, fir 2 x 4's, rubber tires, old oil. The door was open and he could see the yard and road but no one could see him; the garage was like a large shadowy room, filled with interesting furniture.

Sometimes when he was alone, thinking of the future and all the things that were possible, he got a quivery feeling up his back: there was only one of him, he was like no other person. To focus on himself made him tremble self-consciously.

Feeling the pleasure of being alone, he spit in the dust, a fine powder pulverized by years of being walked on, and saw it close around his spit. He loved the confusion of things the garage contained. On the workbench were tools, spread like cards thrown into the air, and some of his father's eternal projects: a broken toaster, a radio chassis out of the case, a disassembled carburetor, a kerosene lantern fitted with an electric light bulb socket. Toward the back were old wooden cigar boxes filled with carriage bolts, washers, nuts, metal screws, hinges, staples, pins.

Under the bench were the boxes Chris especially enjoyed: they contained things which his father felt might someday become useful, such as assorted used nuts and bolts, obsolete spark plugs, small brass nozzles, nipples, petcocks, zerk fittings, obscure parts from obscure cars and cycles. There were boxes of old Teamster union pins, Oregon license plates, carb jets, brake rivets, cotter keys, axle keys, padlocks, wrenches with their jaws worn smooth, worn drill bits, a fancy wooden-handled jack knife with broken blades, part of a caliper, and a thousand objects which probably no one could identify. He loved to sort through the boxes, feel the weight and textures of metal and wood worn smooth. He felt quivery when he thought about those boxes being here through the years, waiting to be somehow used while he went through his daily routine.

The Weasel

He saw the movement at the end of the log pile and stopped, rifle at his side. From the corner of his eye he could see Horace below and a little to the rear, crossing the grassy space which separated the cemetery from the woods.

Earlier they had entered the old part of the cemetery, had climbed past the huge, ornate, monolithic gravestones, past the mausoleum, past the two silver howitzers, past the military burial section, and into the newer area where all tombstones were sunk below the level of the grass. Once the cemetery had ended well before the reservoir; now bulldozed areas had eaten away tall firs to make room for more graves.

When they had reached the reservoir they had put the clips into their rifles and a shell in the breech. Although the topography around the woods had been changed, Chris and Horace, from habit, sought out the familiar trail above the reservoir which led into the dark woods. When he was on the trail Chris began to feel more at ease, but his breath came quickly; he didn't know whether this was because of the excitement he felt or the exertion of climbing the mountain.

Workmen had left a pile of logs beside the path, and as Chris approached he saw movement at the end of the logs. He froze, eyes on the spot, until a small head appeared over the top log. Slowly he raised the rifle muzzle, his body controlling the gun until he could see in his mind a silhouette of the gold front bead laid on the black outline of the head.

He fired from the hip and the animal disappeared.

When he went to the logs and looked over the side he saw the long, thin body, barely attached to a sharp head. The eyes were covered with a translucent film, and the front teeth looked vicious.

"What is it?" Horace asked.

Chris poked the animal with his toe. "Dunno. Not a squirrel. Not a gopher." He had seen gophers in North Dakota.

"Maybe a mink," Horace said. "Or a weasel."

"That's what it is," Chris said, wanting it to be a weasel or some predator. All he knew for sure was that he had had a target about the size of a half-dollar and that he had hit the animal square in the neck from a distance of thirty feet firing from the hip. He was excited by and in awe of the magic of the act.

Snack

Because it was Saturday night and everyone else had gone to the store, he poked around in the refrigerator looking for a treat, something to eat while he listened to the radio. They never bought frivolous things, like the cases of Coke or Hires which sat on the back porch at Buzz's house, they hardly ever bought potato chips or Cheesits, never had things he thought of as exotic such as coconuts, fresh pineapple, pomegranates, Ghirardelli chocolate, and so he was surprised to find the sausage.

It was three times as big as a wiener, and was flecked with black peppercorns. He placed the sausage on a fork and slowly heated it over the gas stove until it began to swell and split, the juices sputtering across the flame.

He carried it and a jar of mustard into the front room and lay on the floor in front of the radio. Gangbusters had just begun: the sound of a police siren, the chatter of a machine gun, and the tramp of marching feet. "Gangbusters, a Phillips H. Lord production .... "

The comic books were in two piles, recently read and not recently read. From the unread pile he took an old *Airboy,* and as he read and listened to the radio he bit into the tough skin, sucked at the juices. Slowly he nibbled around the end, taking mouse-size bites. When he had worked back a half inch he got up, went into the kitchen and while listening to the radio narrative he re-heated the end of the sausage until it became dark and juicy. Back in the front room he dipped the sausage into the jar of mustard and slowly nibbled.

He stopped reading and listened attentively to the wanted section at the end of the program. "Wanted: Melvin Lewis for murder, twenty seven years old, five feet eight inches tall .... " He listened, wondering whether he had ever seen this man, trying to picture him from the description given over the radio; as always, he felt a shiver of terror when he thought of the hunted man hiding outside his own window, watching him at this very

48

minute. "If you have seen this man, notify the FBI, your local law enforcement agency, or Gangbusters, at once!"

He turned the radio dial to another station to get the FBI in Peace and War, corning in on the hypnotically insistent theme music, "L-A-V-A, L-A-V-A." He had eaten only a fourth of the sausage, and he could see that it would last through The Vaughn Monroe Show, The Perry Como show, Mystery Theater, the news, and until he had to go to bed.

Goodwill

"Rags for the riff-raff," Horace said, hoisting a flannel shirt delicately with two fingers and letting it fall back. "Clothes for the Unclean, the lepers of Lents." They were uneasy in the store, and therefore disdainful; they hoped that they wouldn't see anyone they knew.

An old woman looked at them over the tops of her glasses, and Horace moved on, shoulders hunched forward, a foolish grin spreading. Chris tried to not breathe, for the Goodwill store had the odor of mustiness, mothballs, of other lives.

Racks of threadbare overcoats, dull suits, frayed clothing; tables loaded with terra-cotta dogs, salt and pepper shakers, over-size lamps, chipped dishes, tooth-notched silverware; an endless line of old shoes, toes turned up at the world. Chris and Horace loved old stuff, but there was nothing in the Goodwill worthy of their affection, except some of the hardware.

They stopped near the cardboard boxes of junk, where small wheels were piled. "Here's a nice one," Horace said, laughing, holding up an old baby-buggy wheel with its spokes bent and broken. He cast it aside disdainfully. The next one was a solid wagon wheel with good rubber; using his finger as an axle, he spun it to check the bearings. "Hmmmmm," he said. Then he searched for three others like it, spreading the rejects over the floor.

"Here's a good one that's different," he said. "Want it?"

"I got some at home," Chris said. He was putting aside money for high school clothes, and so he was, as usual, almost broke; he did have a set of wheels on a push-cart that his father had built for him long ago.

When Horace found four wheels he paid the woman at the junk-laden main desk and they fell out into the sunshine, breathing deeply, laughing about the worthless merchandise of the Goodwill.

"Jeez," Chris said, "what a lot of derbis."

"Derbis," Horace laughed, snuffling through his nose. "Derbis. You mean, debris? *debree?*"

"Uh, yah," Chris said, turning the word around in his mind. The spelling didn't seem right, but he bowed to Horace's knowledge of such things. Since he had been running around with Horace he had been using bigger words, and it bothered him when he misused them. Like *orge* when he meant *ogre.* "You know what I mean."

Lents was quiet, and it seemed almost like a Sunday: there was no traffic, plenty of parking space, and few people on the sidewalks. The place had a nice sleepy feeling, Chris thought, the sun mellowing along his shoulders. He imagined that this was what Lents had probably looked like years before. Somewhere in the dust a large grey grasshopper made a clacking sound.

They crossed the street kitty-corner and stopped before the Aero to study the posters; the films were *They Made Me a Criminal* with John Garfield and *Wake Island.* From the Rose Lantern came the salty odor of beer and a woman's hoarse laughter. Chris looked up at the single row of windows; he had once thought that gypsies lived there, and even now he sensed that strange dramas went on in those boxy, stale-smelling apartments. What would it be like to live over a tavern? he wondered.

They walked through the sleepy heat to the Mt. Scott drugstore where they bought ice-cream cones, which they carried to the magazine rack. Sometimes they bought phosphates and took the comics to the fountain, but that was risky; the manager always kept an eye open for freeloaders.

They ducked low behind the greeting cards and slowly licked their cones while they read. Chris got through the new *Tarzan, Real Clue,* and *Detective* comics, and was halfway through *Airboy* when the pharmacist appeared at the top of the card rack.

"That's enough now, boys," he said. "This isn't a lending library, you know."

"Okay," said Chris, starting to put back the comic book.

The man moved away again and Chris continued to read; he'd finished by the time the man came back again. "I've told you boys at least a dozen times. This isn't a lending library."

Horace pushed his glasses back on his nose and snorted; when he got up he was still in the stooped position of sitting. Chris laughed uneasily, feeling conspicuous. When they got to the door they both started laughing—they'd never thought it was a lending library.

The Mistake

"Crap," his father said. "So what'd you do, cut the wheels and axles off?" The pushcar was on its side against the garage wall, the red paint gone from the wooden parts where Chris had done the cutting.

"Yeah," he said, ashamed of what he had done, and feeling confused. He needed the axles and wheels for his racer, and anyway he never used the push car anymore. The idea had seemed a good one until his father had gone into the garage.

"With an *ax?*" his father said.

Chris started to get angry at the questioning, and then he felt sad; his father had made the pushcar for him when Chris had been four or five years old, when they didn't have any money for toys or presents. It was a flat board with four wheels, and it had a handle you pushed backward and forward to make the car go. It had taken his father days of work to build it, and now the pushcar was pretty well shot.

112th Street Hill

The road was a long black asphalt slide ahead of the car.

He looked down the steep incline and was pleasantly scared. He didn't want to go down, really, but it had taken forever to pull the racer to the top of the hill and now there was no other way.

He sat on the box which was the seat, and adjusted the steering ropes. The sun reflected off the road, sending up shimmering waves that distorted the creek beyond; from all sides came the overpowering odor of blackberries. From here he could see over the tops of the high firs, to the house and Lents. In front of him the road seemed to drop forever.

They had begun early this morning, pulling the racers over dusty roads toward Foster Road, struggling with every bump, and finally the long trek up to Mt. Scott to this vantage point. Because his was heavier–too heavy, he knew–he was exhausted by the time they reached the top. He had built the frame from planks, and the blunt radiator was a solid piece of fir. He had nailed on a nameplate from one of his father's machines, Hercules Diesel, which was in keeping with its trucklike appearance; he had named it Sweet Sixteen. Horace had built his of lath struts covered with a white sheet; not only was it lighter, it was also streamlined.

They had made several short runs from lower points on the hill, and then they had thrown themselves into the tall grass beside the road and opened their lunch sacks. As they ate they compared experiences, recalling how fast one car had gone or how close it had veered to the edge or how well the brakes had worked.

Now they were ready for the big run of the day. Chris adjusted the steering rope, and pulled his father's motorcycle goggles over his eyes. "Contact," he said, and Horace kicked the block from under the rear wheel. Slowly the racer began to inch forward, the wheels barely turning, each spoke moving like the second hand on a clock.

The car picked up speed, and within the space of fifteen feet it moved at a comfortable pace. As the momentum increased the buggy wheels bounced against the rough pavement and it was all Chris could do to keep tension in the rope to hold the car straight. He thought of Tazio Nuvolari, steering with only the top of the post, pounding on the door for more speed as he went on to win. Chris loved this sense of movement, speed, the wind rushing past without effort on his part.

Under him the box pounded against his seat with every small bump, and he leaned forward, struggling with the ropes, as the ground rushed past. He was really moving now–the spokes were a blur–and he began to wonder whether he would be able to stop at the bottom before he went into Johnson Creek. He glanced at the brake–a two by four nailed to the frame–and saw that vibrations had loosened it; unable to take his hands from the ropes to grab the handle, he saw it hit the pavement and fly into the air, far over his head.

He was halfway down the hill and travelling fast. Slowly the car began to swerve, drifting toward the edge; he pulled on the rope, like a man trying to rein in a runaway. The car was too heavy: a front wheel began to warp, wobble, spokes separated from the rim; the car slid to the left, then the right, covering the entire road.

Holding tightly to the useless ropes, as if he could pull the car to a stop, he saw over the hood the giant oak; it was the only real obstacle on the descent and he was aimed directly at it. Earlier he had told himself he would jump, but now such action seemed impossible; the car was going too fast.

Then he was off the road and slowly, with incredible clarity, he felt the car tipping, felt himself going over, floating through air. It was like a dream. He tasted the dry, stiff summer grass, and felt the air go out of him. High overhead he saw the racer, hanging like a black weight.

He sat up, gasping for breath, waiting for any pain which would indicate a broken bone. He looked one way and saw the racer, upside down, at the foot of the oak tree; he looked the other way and saw the thin streak his demolished wheel had cut in the road.

He got to his feet, laughing: the car had shot off the road, overturned, dumped him, and rolled–how many times? four? five? He was laughing as he looked far up the hill to where Horace waited, a small figure beside the white racer, and he knew that this would be a story he would tell a dozen times during the following week.

Breaking Windows

Alan Ladd as Whispering Smith sat far back in the boxcar, pistol drawn, the footsteps overhead coming closer, and Chris scrunched down in his seat, involved in the dangers on the screen but aware that outside the theater door Mal waited to be admitted. Tension grew as the footsteps on the screen approached. Near the front of the theater a match flared, went out. The Lents Gang sat there. Over the heads he could see The Flynn's sailor cap tilted far back on the wave of hair. Boozer had his tattooed arm around a girl, probably Dorothy. The movie faces grew larger. Staples which had been shot into the screen by rubber bands looked like facial blemishes.

Chris sat in the first row of the middle aisle, up against the wall by the exit, and when the screen darkened to an inside view of the boxcar he reluctantly got up and went through the curtains which shrouded the door. When the shooting began he pushed the steel bar which locked the exit, shoved a piece of cardboard against the catch, and slipped back through the curtain to his seat. Gunplay on the screen had muffled any sounds he might have made, and the darkened boxcar muted the theater's light.

He began to breathe more easily; guns flashed as he got up and walked, casually he hoped, toward the lobby. He wanted to be away from that row if there was trouble. As he looked down the aisle he saw Mal slip through the curtains into the seat Chris had just left. Alan Ladd emptied his Colt .44 Frontier model toward the boxcar's roof.

The lobby smelled of popcorn and Lysol, perfume and beer, cigarette smoke and moldy rug. Chris stood before the candy counter surveying the Ju-Ju's, Black Crows, Dots, Good 'n

Plentys, 5th Avenue bars while the pimply-faced high school girl hummed a popular tune and looked in other directions for boys her own age. On Friday nights the theater had a good crowd: men in shiny suits, women with bandanas, farmers in overalls who had driven in from as far away as Boring and Happy Valley stood along the walls waiting for this feature to end while their children played on the worn carpet or clustered near the curtains to see the screen's action.

From the corner of his eye Chris saw Mal push through the crowd of kids and move along the wall toward the drinking fountain; he took a drink and as he wiped his chin he surveyed the lobby. Apparently satisfied that he had not been observed, he crossed over to Chris.

"Hey, howya doing?" he said, pretending he hadn't expected to run into Chris. He punched him gently on the shoulder. "When'd you get here? I been here about an hour, didn't see you." He pulled a dime from his pocket. "Lemme have a couple O. Henry bars, sis."

He gave one to Chris, who had used his own quarter to get them into the theater, and they started toward the curtained aisle when Chris felt a hand tightly grip his arm.

"Who sold you guys tickets?" It was Bratt, the owner, and his brown suit bunched up as he steered them toward the front door. "I told you not to come back."

"What'd we do?" Chris asked.

Children stopped playing. In the faces of the people who lined the lobby Chris could see displeasure and self-righteous anger and morbid curiosity. Bratt's adult strength moved them across the worn rug.

"I told you two the last time," Bratt said, his face red and sweaty. He pushed them out the wide doors, and from the security of his theater he repeated the warning. "I mean it, don't come back."

"What'd we do?" Mal asked. "You have to tell us our crime." Mal had been in most kinds of trouble and he figured that qualified him as an expert on the law. Bratt shut the door and

Mal laughed, brushing the hair out of his eyes. "That guy's so dull he couldn't cut hot butter."

"Rats," Chris said. It was bad enough to be kicked out for a reason, but to be kicked out for no reason was worse. He had lost the quarter it cost him to get in, and now he was broke. It was apparent that Bratt had mistaken them for someone else. For the next month, until Bratt forgot about him or whoever he thought Chris was, he'd have to be careful around this theater; he didn't have the money to get to the Bob White.

"Hell's bells, don't get pissed," Mal said. "C'mon, let's look for an adventure."

"Yeah, but you didn't lose two-bits," Chris said, feeling the loss. They stood under the tall theater posters advertising *Whispering Smith,* and Chris wondered how the film ended; he figured that he would never know, because films began in downtown Portland and worked their way into the suburbs, and the Aero was the last to get any film. What seemed an inexplicable puzzle bothered him more than the loss of the money.

"Two-bits, two shmitz," Mal said. "C'mon."

Music poured from the open doorway of the Rose Lantern, and over it came the sound of a woman's shrill laughter. The air was filled with the salty odor of beer, like an ocean breeze. Across the street two toughs lounged against the window of the Coney Island talking with two girls; one guy Chris recognized as Jergens. On most nights Lents was dead, the streets empty, stores dark, but tonight there was an electric excitement: laughter, lights, the music of juke-boxes and upstairs apartments, tires screaming away from the stop-light. At the Coney Island a girl laughed, shoved the sleeves of her sweater up to her elbows, swung sideways until the thin pleats of her bright Pendleton skirt were a blur. Overhead the Aero's purple neon marquee pulsed against the night.

"I got an idea," Mal said, turning the corner and walking down Woodstock. The street here was deserted and dark. At the same exit door Chris had opened for him a few minutes earlier, Mal stopped, began to scream and beat on the door with his fists, and then he started running. Chris took off, expecting Bratt to come through that door and catch him. He followed Mal to the corner, avoided the garbage can that Mal had knocked over, and together they cut up the alley to Foster Road. Breathless, they ducked behind a parked car at the body shop and waited, suppressing laughter. No one came, but Chris had to admit he did feel better. He knew what the sound of someone beating on the theater door was like inside the theater, especially during certain tender moments on the screen.

"Ah, hell," Mal said, and he threw a beer bottle down the alley; air droned across its mouth and then the tinkle of broken glass. "Hell's bells," he said, brushing the hair from his eyes.

They walked along Foster to 92nd, Chris looking over his shoulder, and stood in the light of Mt. Scott Drugstore; the fountain was doing a thriving business. They waited, while Chris watched in every direction for pursuers; it seemed that he and Mal were always being chased by someone, and lately he had begun to worry about getting caught. "Want to read some comic books?" he asked.

"Hell no," Mal said. "C'mon." Chris knew that Mal wanted to find adventure, and he followed him across the street to the Rexall Pharmacy where they leaned against the wall. A bus stopped with a hiss of air brakes, let on an old woman, and took off again, sparks flying from the overhead runners. Lights went out in Butterfield's Grocery. A coupe with dual exhausts rumbled to a stop, and took off. Sharp laughter came from Reilly's Tavern, and a little farther down and across the street singing came from the house which was the converted Negro church. Bob Mountain lurched into the tavern's neon, wiped his nose with a bandana, and lurched homeward.

"Hey," said Mal, as if it were the most reasonable thing in the world, "you want to roll a drunk?"

Chris trembled: the idea appealed to him and terrified him.

He couldn't imagine wrestling with a guy like Bob Mountain, who was huge and a crazy Indian to boot. He had *read* about people rolling drunks and it never seemed very difficult in books.

"How would you do it?"

"You got the alley by the hardware store, or the one by Farah's store. Get a drunk into the alley and hit him on the head. Most of these guys are so looped they're almost out anyway."

"How'd you know if they got any money?" Chris asked, as if he were looking for a reason to not go through with the plan.

"Money, shmoney," Mal said, brushing his hair back.

"C'mon, let's see how the street looks from above." He moved quickly down the block, past Reilly's dimly lit windows, the closed stores, the darkened alley, and crossed the street. Music swelled in the night behind the high laurel hedge which screened the Negro church. Ramona Street ended at 92nd and where there would have been a street there was the Masonic Lodge. They climbed the wooden stairs which served as a fire escape, and at the second floor landing they climbed a ladder to the roof.

Tar still reeked of the day's heat, and reflected the blackness of the sky. At the edge they looked down 92nd Street, from the darkened stores to the lighted taverns to the Aero's neon marquee two blocks away. Dance music came from the building under them, and gospel music from the Negro church next door. A new Buick raced away from the stoplight toward the city's limits. Because this was Friday night a muted, festive spirit hung in the air over Lents, like a party which was ending or which just could never quite get started.

A kid on a bike pumped past; from this angle Chris could not identify him. A figure struggled out of the alley and walked in tiny, unsteady steps toward the intersection. "Old Man Mountain," Chris said. He could see the gunny sack hung over the man's back; Old Man Mountain, Bob Mountain's father, always carried a gunny sack. Buzz claimed it was filled with skunk cabbage. "No money there."

Another man staggered out the door, across the curb; he rested against a car fender, and then started down the street. Chris felt his guts tighten. "Let's get him," Mal said. But the man turned and went back into the tavern. Two minutes later he came out again, stood around on the sidewalk, and went back in as if he couldn't make up his mind.

They watched the deserted street until Mal grew tired and rolled on his side, picking at the asphalt out of boredom. "Hell's bells, a jack-roller'd starve around this place."

Chris felt a gnawing excitement simply in seeing the street at this hour from this angle, and as the tempo of the music from the Negro church grew he felt something building within him. He thought of Tom and Huck peering into the robbers' house on the island, or observing their own funerals.

"Listen to them jigs," Mal said. The music grew louder and they could hear the voice of the preacher in a booming counterpoint and people shouting over and over, "Amen, amen, brother." It reminded him of the Lents Evangelical United Brethren church. But Chris's church was in plain sight; the Negro church was hidden in an old house behind a tall laurel hedge and boxed in by commercial buildings. Chris had seen the house once, but he had never seen the worshippers; so far as he knew no Negroes lived in or around Lents, except for Nigger Tom who drove down from Mt. Scott in a wagon pulled by two horses as worn and as black as himself.

"Hang on." Chris heard Mal's steps scuff across the flat roof and he waited in darkness. Then Mal was back. "Here," he said, shoving the white package into Chris's hand. A roll of toilet paper. Mal had known where to find it in this building, in the same way that he knew where the best dill pickles and bamboo and canned fruit could be stolen. He knew Lents like the back of his hand. "Peel off a strip, stand on it, and give the roll a toss." He followed his own instructions and the roll sailed high overhead, a white streak fluttering across the night, to land in the English walnut tree outside the church where it bounced from limb to limb. Chris threw his roll, and although the streamer broke in mid-air the paper unfurled across the sky and fell into the same tree, dispersing itself.

"Those jigs'll crap," Mal said, laughing. "C'mon, we can get a couple more out of the women's john." They ran across the roof and down the ladder to the second floor landing. The window was open and they found themselves in a hallway off the dance floor. Mal knocked, listened, then opened the door. "Stand guard. Knock twice if somebody comes."

Chris was nervous in the hallway. The music, a waltz, seemed to come closer, as if it were part of a parade. What would he do if some women came around the corner–knock twice, then dash for the men's john across the hall, or open the window behind him? When he looked back he saw a girl about his own age coming toward him, wearing a red formal dress with wide skirts. He stiffened, felt his heart jump when he recognized the girl as one he'd seen often at church. She had on high heels, which made her seem taller as well as older. He wanted to knock on the door and run.

"Hi," she said, smiling.

"Hi." Her skirts rustled as she walked, and did he imagine that he heard the sound of her nylons rubbing?

"It's a nice night, isn't it?"

"Uh, yeah. Not bad," he said. He could smell her perfume, see the light tinge of lipstick. Most of the girls at the church never wore makeup. He wanted to run; he wanted to talk with her.

"We've got a real good band," she said, pointing into the room beyond the hall.

Was she inviting him in? he wondered, and looked down at his worn jeans and beat-up shoes. Or was she simply waiting for him to get out of the way, so that she could get through the door to the women's john that he was standing in front of?

"Yeah, it sounds good." He moved away from the door, thinking how hard it was to talk with girls; the conversations of his fantasies all disintegrated when he was confronted by the real thing.

He saw her look of surprise before he heard Mal open the door and step into the hallway, a roll of toilet paper in each hand. "Hiya, sis," he said, motioning with one roll. "C'mon, Little Beaver, let's scratch gravel."

"So long," Chris said, and without waiting for her reply he followed Mal down the hall to the window. As he looked back he saw her standing in the hallway, her skirt spread like a butterfly's wings against the stark white walls. She had never questioned what he was doing there. He followed Mal down the fire escape to the parking lot, wondering if he wanted to see her again at church or if he never wanted to see her again.

At the fire station's driveway Mal unfurled one roll and tossed it into the fish pond, where it slowly became a saturated mess. Across the street he swung the other roll upward in a wide arc and it fell into the corner tree, bouncing from limb to limb. They crossed 92nd and entered the darkness of Lents School playground; Chris had to walk quickly to keep up with Mal, who no doubt figured that the girl had called the police.

Lents School was grim and forbidding against the night, its board sides shedding their last paint until it was like a dark gray monolith three stories high. Chris's class had been the last to graduate from the old school; a new single story school had been built on 97th street and would open in the fall. As they passed between the school and the old wood-working shop, Chris was thinking how he would like to ask that girl out for a date—he had never had a date, but he could ask if she'd like to go to a movie. Then he remembered that he'd been banished from the Aero. Could they go on the bus to the Bob White?

He could barely see Mal, a shadow bent near the ground.

Both 92nd and Harold Streets were empty of traffic, and the only light came from two blocks away. Chris felt funny being in the schoolyard late at night; the place where he had spent so much time over the past nine years looked strange and forbidding at this hour. The building rose beside them, dark and sinister.

"You find any rocks?" Mal asked.

Chris searched at the base of the huge maple tree near the woodshop, his fingers trailing through the dust until they closed on throwing-size stones. He wanted to break a window and yet the idea scared him, but he told himself that he had as much right as anyone to break windows in the school he had attended for nine years; Mal had attended it for only a year or two, before he had moved out of the district.

"When I count three."

Mal counted, and Chris tried to see through the darkness to a target; the tension grew, the buildings grew fuzzy. At three he threw as hard as he could; he heard one hit the wooden side, heard another shatter a window which seemed to break forever, the pieces falling to the cement below where they shattered again, the sound of breaking glass incredibly loud in the sleeping neighborhood. Chris was already running when Mal bumped into him, saying, "Let's get," and they both took off in a dead run across the playground, across Harold Street, and followed the path up the hill through the stand of firs and into the old orchard where they threw themselves into the tall grass, gasping and quietly laughing.

Sands of Time

He turned the radio volume up and went to sit on the front steps. In the east the moon was full but surrounded by a haze, which gave the night a strange feeling. He could see lights in houses along the street, but even as he watched they began to blink out. Between houses were gardens and vacant lots; to the east were empty fields overgrown with Scotch Broom and Oregon Grape. The dark street was desolate and empty. The nearest arc light, a block away, cast a pale circle; no kids played baseball or tag under it. He felt that he had now outgrown those games.

The program ended, signing off with "Ahhhh, Cisco. Ahhhhh, Pancho," the way that Teddy Gaff and Dick Issari said it. A new program began and the announcer's voice conjured the sands of time, the desert, pyramids, a crescent moon. When he spoke of days being as numerous as grains of sand or of the infinity of the galaxy, Chris felt dizzy. It was beyond comprehension. A single day was loaded with events; a year seemed to stretch forever. His parents' lives extended back into times he could barely imagine–tall square cars, heavy dark furniture, rutted roads.

A recurrent image appeared: in the country, under a full moon and a wide summer sky, a boy and a girl sat in a 1940 Ford convertible. They seemed to have just come from a dance; he wore a white suit, and she a frilly dress. She had blonde hair and freckles. In a way they looked like his idea of high school students, or people in the Coke ads over the fountain counter at the Rexall, or pictures in *Collier's*.

The moon glinted off the chrome of his father's car. He got up from the steps and stood beside it, then got in. The dome light flashed and went out when he closed the door. He held the huge white wheel in his hands, steering it over strange roads, and shifted the gear lever. He dreamed of speed–the wind in his face, the effortless thrill of movement, like coasting on his bike or a soapbox racer down an endless hill. If he could get a cheap car and fix it up–or even a Cushman scooter or a Doodlebug, an engine attached to wheels until in his mind the machinery became an extension of himself. In this dream he was moving, freewheeling through time and space.

Phosphate

When the fountain girl turned toward the cash register, Mal reached around the syrup dispensers and got the phosphate. The bottle was small, but the liquid was so powerful the few ounces would probably last for months. A phosphate cost the same as a nickel Coke, but was bigger, and they came in several flavors: cherry, lime, vanilla, root beer, even chocolate.

Mal shook some into his drink, then passed the bottle to Martin, who passed it to Chris. The fountain girl had put the right amount in when she had made it, but they had created a game to see who could stand the most. Like a scientist adding ingredient X, Chris carefully tilted the bottle until two clear drops fell into his glass; he stirred the frothy chocolate and took a drink. Too bitter! The phosphate was like sulfuric acid!

"Hey, Chris," Mal said, "there's that queer Horace." Chris looked up and saw Horace's head bobbing along beyond the window displays. He was slumped forward, eyes on the ground, as if deep in thought.

"Who's that kid?" Harlan asked. "I seen him around."

"Oh, some pud," Mal said, swiveling on his stool.

Chris took another sip of the phosphate and from the corner of his eye he saw Horace lean against the glass doors and enter the drug store, heading for the magazine section. When Horace passed within a few feet Chris started to say something, then turned back to his bitter drink.

The Dream

He stood beside his father on the back steps and they searched the sky. Then he saw it streaking across the northern night: a glint of silver, barely perceptible. It fell from sight, and a moment later the sky was lit with a series of brilliant flashes. "Well," his father said, "there goes Seattle."

He woke from the recurrent dream to the sound of his heart racing. It was always incredibly real–after he woke he could still see the flashes against his eye-lids, as if they'd been seared. It was real because the threat was real; almost every day he thought about the dangers, saw that mushroom-shaped cloud blossom from newsreels. He'd read in *Astounding* how radiation sickness killed those who survived the blast, imagined the victims with the green mucous running from their facial openings. He knew that any survivors would exist as mutants in a barren, radioactive world, and this vision terrified him almost as much as death.

Because of this, he had made lists and drawings, and had his plan for survival. He was prepared to go to the mountains at the first sign of A-bomb attack–alone, if necessary, armed with his rifle and pistol. He had a carton of 500 bullets, a knapsack filled with army surplus K-rations, medicine kit, halizone tablets, mirror, wax-covered matches, etc. In a drawing he wore an Australian bush hat pinned up on one side and topped with a feather. He envisioned a rough, but free life for himself in the woods–hunting, fishing, trapping, building a cabin, living off the land–and he was prepared to stay there for the rest of his life, if necessary.

He shut his eyes and turned over, pulling the blankets tightly against himself, against the darkness. Far away, the Galloping Goose clattered steel on steel.

The Hideout

Walking back from Horace's house, Chris heard voices deep within the bushes. There was no traffic on these rutted back roads, where Scotch Broom and blackberry vines grew in a tangled confusion which sprawled outward until the road became a path, and he stood listening to the muted words. Parting the thick brush he moved closer; then he recognized Harlan's voice. There was the sound of dirt being shoveled, and wood striking wood. Chris crawled forward on his hands and knees and when he parted the brush he saw an area had been cleared and there was fresh dirt piled hip-high.

"Hey," he said, "what's going on?"

"Oh jeezus," Harlan said. He leaned on a shovel, his white T-shirt streaked with dirt. "Beat it. Scratch gravel."

"Who is it?" Martin's head emerged from a hole at Harlan's feet and he looked around. "Beat it, boah. This's a private club."

Chris stood up and walked around the outline of the excavation and when he got back to the hole he tried to see into it. "Oh, c'mon. I won't tell anyone. I promise." The hole obviously led into something.

"No!" said Harlan.

"Shag ass!" said Martin.

Chris persisted until they gave in. Harlan leaned on his shovel, chewed his gum thoughtfully, and said to Martin, "Okay, let him take a look. But remember, kid, you ain't a member."

"Yeah, boah," Martin said, moving back. "You're just a visitor. Tell anyone about this and we'll nut you."

Chris squeezed through the hole and wiggled down a short tunnel; when the ground fell away beneath his legs he turned

65

around. Through the smoky air he could see that they had dug, by hand, a huge room in the earth, almost large enough to stand up in; they had covered the roof with a sliding garage door they had stolen somewhere, and covered that with dirt. When the grass grew back it would be a very secret place.

A candle burned on a wooden box, barely illuminating the dark walls; the smoke curled upward and flattened against the low roof, making Chris's eyes water. On the dirt floor there was an Oriental rug, and on a shelf cut into the wall there was an alarm clock, a carton of Camels, and a pair of binoculars. In the corner Mal and Verlyn were passing a cigarette between them.

"Cripes, where'd you get all this?" Chris was peeved at having been excluded from the club—he'd probably passed right by a dozen times while the work was going on—but he was also amazed at the club's accomplishments.

"Where'd you think?"

"We bought 'em," Martin said sarcastically, trying to stand tall in the low-ceiling room. "Got 'em at the store, boah."

"What a place," Chris said, ignoring Martin. This was their hideout: they could hold secret meetings here, get together with friends, hide any loot that they couldn't take home. It was the kind of place he had always dreamed of having; it was like Tom's secret cave, or: the hillocks in Sherwood Forest where the dwarf archers lived. He sat down near the entrance, his back to the wall, and listened to Harlan shovel dirt on the roof—it was the pleasant sound of rain.

Pantsed

"Jeezus," Harlan said, "who the hell cut the cheese?"

"Ole fart-face there did."

"Up yours."

"Gonna git a little, off-hand?"

"Horse-pucky."

They sat in the near-dark of the hideout exchanging insults and laughing, plotting minor crimes, passing the time.

Thin cracks of light filtered from around the edges of the roof, to reveal the small table made of a drawer turned on its top with a rug thrown over it, and around it five figures squatting against the dark earth walls.

"You cut the cheese, Martin?" Harlan asked.

"Sheet, boah."

"Gimme a butt," Mal said.

"Go flog your dong," Verlyn said. But he took an open pack from the table and shook out one cigarette. For a brief second the match illuminated the small room, the faces tinged with shadow and orange light, and in the afterglow the darkness was complete. The cigarette glowed; smoke rose to the close ceiling and hung there.

"Gimme that cancer stick," Chris said.

"Boah, you don't know shit from shinola," Martin said.

"If brains was dynamite he wouldn't have enough to blow his nose!" Mal said.

"Martin, you pud," Chris said.

"Howzat?" Martin asked.

The cigarette came around the circle to Chris and he raised it to his lips: the solid weight, damp end, the taste of slightly wet tobacco and the smoke which he could not see. He sucked, felt the harshness, exhaled, passed it on. The smoke had hardly hit his lungs when his heart began to race. The crowded, smoky room closed in on him.

"You molest me, you pud," Chris said.

"I what?"

This was the surest way to insult Martin. They had argued about the meaning of the word, which Martin had read in the newspaper and thought was a synonym for rape. "You molest me," Chris repeated, laughing and scared, his heart pounding with the tobacco and the thrill of the chase.

"You're gonna be pantsed, boah, unless you take that back." He rose up in the smoky dark, hunched forward, and grabbed Chris by the legs, pulling him away from the tunnel's opening. Chris felt the dark earth slip through his fingers, tasted its dampness as he tried to scramble loose, but it was no use; Martin was bigger and older, and his weight pinned Chris as his fingers yanked the jeans down, over his shoes, off. The tunnel door let in a flash of light as Martin opened it, threw Chris's pants out into the bushes, and closed it.

"You're gonna get pantsed every time you say that, boah."

Chris stood up, brushed dirt off his underwear and bare legs, and said in a barely audible voice: "You molest me."

Exploring

The door was open.

"C'mon," Horace said, giggling, holding open the door through which they had passed a million times coming from the playground. "Let's check it out."

They stood within the cool shadow of the alcove at the rear of the school; on one side was the grassless playground, where huge dusty-brown grasshoppers clacked with urgency in the hot sun, and on the other side the black maw of the open door.

After circling the empty school building, testing every door, they had found this one open. "C'mon," Horace said again, peering up the darkened stairway as if it were the abandoned fort in *Beau Geste*.

Chris looked around the serrated cement column and listened—the empty streets, the dusty playground, grasshoppers—and then he turned and entered the school.

The stairwell was dark and they waited until the familiar objects materialized: the oak bannister, the narrow tongue and–groove paneling, the foot-worn steps. The school had been in use for over fifty years, and soon it would be demolished.

As he followed Horace up the half-flight of stairs, barely breathing, Chris thought *how familiar everything was!* Nine years spent in this building! Now empty, the place was not much different from when it had been full. Along the side and main halls hung the paintings which had once terrified him: George Washington materializing from the clouds, Roman columns, a pastoral scene of semi-clad picnickers in Olden Days, head shots of stern, unforgiving old men.

The slightest noise echoed against the wooden walls, and Chris was sure he could hear the echo of his pounding heart. The halls smelled of sawdust and linseed oil; how many times had he seen Johnny Johnson ("Yonny Yonson"), the janitor, spread that against the oak boards to clean up a kid's vomit? They stood in the darkness of the main hall, dark at two on a brilliant summer day, and darker than anyone could imagine on a rainy winter day.

Inside, the school was both scary and comfortable. He remembered how after one had arrived at the school one was held in the warm classrooms and protected against wind and rain. Many days he had felt the school was cozy; the poor old cafeteria always spouted forth the delicious odor of hot, homemade tomato soup; the poor old auditorium with its folding wooden chairs brought them together for songs and Christmas plays and sometimes a flickering movie showing Sinbad or Gulliver.

They wandered downstairs and into the gym, whose cement floor had the chill of winter. How many teeth had been chipped or broken on that cement? he wondered, probing with his tongue his own partially missing front tooth. They cautiously pushed open the door to the boys' john, with its strange labyrinth of tall water reservoirs and pipes. Here Bobby Meersham had fallen while jumping from pipe to pipe and had fractured his skull; perhaps, Chris thought, that accident was what had made him a little nutty.

Back upstairs they wandered into familiar rooms and ones they had never entered in all the years between kindergarten and eighth grade: the teachers' room, and the large cubby hole where Mrs. Van Dant kept all the musical instruments. Most rooms were empty, but in the office of Mr. Buffon, the principal, they found two ink bottles. Slowly and with great care Horace opened the caps and dribbled ink across the desk. Then he stood back and giggled.

The action triggered some escape valve: not only would they never have to return to this school, the building wouldn't be here in a few months. Therefore, it was perfectly okay to have their revenge against all the hours they had lived within the confines of these walls, the long afternoons in boring classes when they could have been playing at Indian rock, the hours they had had to stay after school for some minor infraction of the rules, to write upon the blackboard two hundred times "I will not infringe upon the rights of my neighbors" when they could have been sailing rafts along Johnson Creek or hiking up Mt. Scott.

In the main hallway Chris removed the big brass fire extinguisher from its hook and upended the cylinder; a stream of liquid played across the plaster and wood walls, the window with Mr. Buffon, Principal painted on it in black letters, the chairs, and as he walked into the room to spray the chest high wooden partition behind which the secretary, Mrs. Edgington, had always sat, the liquid slowed to a trickle. Chris shook the container, and dropped it in the corner.

They went from room to room spraying the fire extinguishers on everything. They wrote obscene words in liquid on the blackboards. In the room Chris had once had as an Art room the extinguisher refused to work. He shook it, but nothing came out. Then he unscrewed the entire top and found a gray container attached to it. He pressed a finger against it, and suddenly liquid sprayed across his face. It was sharp, biting; he knew the extinguishers worked on the soda acid principle, and he realized that this was the acid. Throwing away the container, he jumped back and hollered, his eyes closed, afraid to open them and afraid to rub them with his hand.

"What the heck?" Horace said, laughing.

"Acid!" Chris said, rubbing his shirt sleeve against his cheek and eyes, spitting the bitter taste which had entered his mouth. He blinked, found he could see, and began to laugh. "I gotta get some water."

The only drinking fountain in the entire school was in the basement, and they went there to wash off the acid. Chris leaned his burning cheek into the trickle and as the coolness washed over him he thought of wet wool jackets and boot socks, the oily odor of yellow rain slickers, of standing safety-patrol in the near-darkness, sack lunches, the corrugated cardboard sheets on which he had taken brief naps in kindergarten, chalk dust, overalls and corduroy, the slick paper of new books, erasers, playing marbles in the muddy ground of spring, looking out the window when the weather was too beautiful for any school day.

"C'mon," Horace called. He was hauling a large block of wood away from Johnny Johnson's furnace room and up the stairs. Chris grabbed one end and they took it to the first floor; Horace lifted the block, rocked his weight back and forth, and let it fly: slowly it tumbled through the air and in slow motion· crashed into and past the glass doors which led to the false balcony. Within the empty building the noise of falling glass echoed endlessly, as if each splinter shattered into sound.

"Oh Christ," Chris said, moving back, "somebody's going to hear that."

Horace laughed. "Give 'em a broadside, clear the decks with grape-shot! "

They shot off more fire extinguishers and broke up chalk.

Chris found a rock on the floor of Mrs. Douglas's room, lying where it had fallen after it had sailed through the window, and threw it into the blackboard. He picked it up and threw it again. After he had made several holes in the board he threw it overhand at a ceiling light; it hit the base and the heavy glass fixture crashed intact to the floor where it disintegrated. Chris started to pick it up again, then stopped.

"You hear something?"

They stiffened, listening; the empty halls were silent.

However, not wanting to be caught in a room they wandered down the hallway to where the main halls intersected. They listened, poised against a silence which was so intense it seemed to have a solid weight. Chris heard the beat and echo of his heart. Horace giggled, shrugged, and walked toward the principal's office; he picked up an empty fire extinguisher canister, raised it overhead, saying, "Death to the infidel!" and was about to throw it through the opaque window when heavy steps sounded along the boards.

"Run!" Chris said, trying to make his legs move as he saw beyond Horace a figure coming around the corner, saw the blue uniform of a fireman, saw Horace drop the canister with an awkward, almost feeble, motion and turn to begin to run, and then his own legs were moving, his feet slipping against the oak floor. *Jeezus!* he thought, scared and thrilled at the same time, running from the shadows into a patch of sunshine and hit the top of the stairs at a dead run, went down them three at a time and kept hoping that another fireman wasn't waiting for them at the bottom, hoping that the door was unlocked, hoping that the fireman wasn't a fast runner.

He hit the door bar with all his weight and it flew open and he was down the six steps to the ground, running as fast as he could, cutting across Harold Street with barely an eye for traffic and running across the field toward The Path. There were fields up there where he could hide, until he had to circle back home for his paper route.

At the tall Douglas firs he slowed and for the first time looked back. No one was in pursuit, nor was Horace following. Chris lay down in the thick clumps of Oregon Grape which grew at the foot of the trees, watching the school ground as he sucked in great lungfuls of air and wondered whether under duress Horace would fink on him.

Sleeping Out

"You're not going to go sleep in any hole out in the field," his mother said, "and that's that!"

"But, mom, all the guys'll be there. Shoot, I'll be the only one who–"

"Look," she said, standing in the doorway with her hands on her hips, "I don't care. You're not going. Fish, who knows what could happen? What if some nut comes by?"

Frustrated by his lack of power and authority over his own life, Chris threw a tantrum. He stomped around and hollered until his father threatened to take a razor strop after him. He went out and sat on the front steps, feeling angry and resentful.

He could see across the fields, dim with the last golden light of dusk, to the place where the hideout was; even now he imagined Martin, Harlan, and the others bedding down for the night, telling stories, smoking a cigarette, and his anger grew. To be cut off from such things simply because he was only thirteen and dependent upon others.

Then he got an idea: he would sleep in his own yard, sneak across the fields after his parents went to bed, and he'd return before dawn. He composed himself and asked if he could sleep in the yard; his parents, no longer angry, said sure.

He spent the next hour and a half listening to the radio and reading comic books, and when the sky was good and dark he brushed his teeth and took his sleeping bag into the yard. Spreading the bag under the willow tree, he took off his shoes and crawled into the bag. Stars danced just beyond the willow's branches; the moon, low in the eastern sky, washed the entire yard with a silvery whiteness which seemed to him almost mystical. Somewhere in the neighborhood a radio was playing Perry Como. The grass had a clean smell, and the bag smelled of moist canvas. He looked at the stars and thought about the desert sands, the pyramids, eternity, about his friends and his parents' friends, and about waking tomorrow and having bacon and eggs in the sunshine and about how time passes, and at some point he fell asleep long before the lights in the house went out.

The next morning he was up early and running across the fields while the dew still sparkled in spider webs. He crawled through the tall Scotch Broom bushes and when he approached the center he saw that someone had kicked in the roof of the hideout. The dirt was thrown back, the hole open to the sunlight, and everything was gone.

Later he learned that the police had been there, called by the lady whose rug, garage door, and digging tools had been stolen and used on the hideout. Everyone had been asleep when the cops had started smashing in the roof, kicking dirt down on the sleepers, and they had roused them out of the hole and made them line up for the search. All the stolen items were taken back by the woman, and the cops, after writing down the boys' names and addresses, told everyone to go home and keep their noses clean.

Within a week neighbors began to dump junk into the hole, and by the following spring it was loaded with rusty cans, lizards, and garter snakes.

The Plane Crash

"Look!" the leader said, braking hard, stopping, pointing up. Bikes slowed to a stop, wheels bounced across the dry grass. They looked upward, toward the plane whose engine began the high-pitched scream they had heard so often in war communiqué films. "The son-of-a-gun is gonna crash," someone said.

They had been riding their bikes around Lents Park, scrambling after each other in a game of chase along the sidewalks, through the tennis courts, and down the steep paths that led to the lower park, and now they braked in the middle of the athletic field on the upper level, looking into the sky. The plane, an old Army trainer, had been stunting for several minutes, doing wide loops and barrel-rolls, and then, as they watched, it seemed to hang in the air nose up. Slowly it dropped on one wing, and they saw—or later thought they had seen—something fall from the plane, a sliver which floated down like a leaf.

They watched as the plane continued toward the ground a few hundred feet below; no one spoke, and the noise of the plane's engine, screaming earthward, seemed to fill the park. Chris held his breath, both fearing and wishing that the plane would crash, but most of all believing that the plane at any minute would pull up, level off, and hurtle back toward the thin summer clouds.

When the plane disappeared behind the trees, they kicked their bikes into action. They rode madly, laughing, excited, stunned by disbelief—the plane *must* have crashed! They raced along 92nd Street until they came to the top of the hill, and looked down where it intersected with Powell Boulevard. They saw the silver cross of the plane nosed into the parking lot of Keelings Cottage—it had missed both the tavern and the busy intersection by only a few feet. Already a crowd was gathering,

74

and as they pumped downhill they heard the sound of a siren. They parked their bikes and entered the throng of dazed motorists and drinkers, moving toward the wreckage. The plane, tail in the air, was only a third its original size.

"No smoking," a man kept yelling, waving his arms as he moved through the crowd; he wore an Ike jacket, and Chris wondered if he had experienced things like this during the war. "There's gas all over! No smoking!"

Wreckage was strewn over the parking lot, and with feverish intensity they began to pick up souvenirs of silver plywood and shattered Plexiglas. As Chris got closer to the plane he looked up to see the man in the rear cockpit, an arm over the side, his face pressed into the instrument panel.

Peaches

All afternoon they worked in the yard, trimming and raking and burning. The air was pleasantly warm and carried the smell of burning wood, like a good fall day. About five o'clock his mother brought out Kool-Aid, wieners, and a bowl of cold pork and beans; they cooked hot dogs in the glowing embers of what they had burned.

He loved days like this. The sun slanted behind the neighbor's house burnishing their own with a rich, golden light, and the wood smoke danced lazily in the rays. Cut grass, smoke, the wiener's juice all merged, and he could barely believe how peaceful the neighborhood was—he felt an acute pleasure in being alive.

When they had finished eating his mother brought out the peaches. He had risked his life to get them. Canned the summer before, they had been in the food locker at Rick's; this was the last container of peaches. Yesterday afternoon, before going on his paper route, Chris had ridden his bike to Rick's store and had braved the frozen death of the locker room: the heavy door had slammed behind him, and he had faced the room which seemed like the inside of an iceberg. Quickly he found their locker, moved the ladder to it, climbed to the highest row of lockers, got the lock opened, found and took out the final quart of peaches, locked the locker, and raced for the door. To his infinite surprise and relief, it swung open. He was sure that someday he would be trapped in that wasteland.

He hated the softness of canned peaches, but if they were crisp through freezing, with slivers of ice imbedded in the pulpy tissue, he loved them.

"So you saw the plane crash?" his father said, looking up from the paper.

"Yep," he said, sucking on a frozen wedge of peach.

"I mean, you actually seen it *hit?*"

Chris had to admit that he hadn't. "When we come over the top of the hill, you know, looking down 92nd, we seen it on the ground. We were somewhere between Holgate and the park when it musta hit."

The crash was a vivid memory: the plane accordianed like a venetian blind fallen to the floor, the arm hanging over the side of the rear cockpit, the smell of gasoline rising like a thick blanket. But more vivid was the sense of falling: the plane tumbling over and over like a weighted leaf, unreal against the blue sky, the awful inevitability of the crash, and the two men faced with no other choice but to jump or ride it down. What would he have done? he wondered.

"Bet those drunks in Keelings Kottage got out fast," his father said, laughing. "Bet there were a few pants to clean afterward."

"I'll bet," Chris said, thinking how close the plane had come to so many people—in the tavern, on Powell, on 92nd—and then thinking how many times he had been at that intersection, in that same parking lot. Suddenly he felt very vulnerable.

His father folded the paper, and carried some dishes toward the house. Chris slowly savored the last peach wedges in his bowl and sucked their coolness; the sensation lingered on his tongue. How pleasant: peach, dusk, a light smoke drifting over the neighborhood like sleep, cut grass smell, somewhere a garden hose playing against cement, a tree frog, the odor of green tomatoes shaking off the day's heat, dimly heard radio voices, dishes clinking, farther off the voices of kids playing, farthest off the long whine of a locomotive at the edge of the world.

He got up and walked to the driveway where his bike was parked, and hardly pedaling he moved easily down the street. The air had the mysterious quality of summer dusk, as if the sky had descended; everything took on a kind of clarity, but when he tried to look directly at an object it became obscured in shadow. Two blocks away some kids were playing baseball at the corner, and their shouts carried across the stillness. He continued to pedal on toward Lents, feeling a pleasure as the tires rolled easily across the cement sidewalk of Ramona Street.

Lents was nearly empty. Old Man Mountain stood outside Reilly's Tavern looking through the window, the gunny sack of skunk cabbages slung over his shoulder. A couple sat at the fountain counter of Mt. Scott Drug Store. A lone car stopped for the flashing red light, and slowly turned the corner; the street was empty all ways.

Chris pedaled slowly toward home, the slight breeze tugging at his T-shirt. The arc light at 97th and Ramona went on, and he remembered how just a few short years before the kids had all decided that it was "officially" night when the street lights went on.

He parked the bike and sat at the table in the backyard, where the embers still glowed in the day's fire. An odd gust of wind tossed the willow tree, flashing the lighter underside of its leaves. He looked beyond the tree to the stars; although the moon had begun to ascend, the sky directly overhead as black, and the blackness was salted with points of light. As the tree moved the sky seemed to move, and he suddenly felt dizzy, staggered by the cosmos, so he climbed onto the table and lay on his back. The dizzyness left him, and now he felt fear: he recognized in rare moments like this how tenuous was the hold one had on life. Leaves fluttering, darkness, the infinity of stars: the old funereal props, and he wondered once again whether his mother or his father would die first. Would he die first? He closed his eyes, tried to force that thought out of his mind, but it kept coming back like the after-image of stars against his eye-lids, and he was still working on it when his mother shouted through the back-porch screen that he had better get ready for bed.

He got ready and later, in his bed, he lay with his hands behind his head staring up at the ceiling; the glow from the radio tubes cast yellow patterns on the walls, and he could smell the odor of dust burning off the tubes. He loved to lie in bed and listen to the radio late at night; the voices gave him a sense of connections, as if to say that he was not all alone in the world.

The ten o'clock news. *Five Star Final-Names Make News and So Do These.* He listened to the international news, and then, taking precedent over several national stories, the announcer mentioned the plane crash. A war-surplus BT 13, which the owner had hoped to sell. He mentioned names, and said that the pilot had jumped at only 500 feet.

After the news came Down Memory Lane, a show which played old music. Chris hated the program, but there was nothing else on that was any good; at 10: 15 on a Sunday night there was St. Francis of Assisi and various other religious programs that he didn't care about. So he listened to the old records, the scratchy antique records which seemed to be from another era, a world which he could barely imagine. The music conjured up an image of the past, a metal fence covered with wild roses which surrounded a small garden; beyond that was an old house, and in a darkened room was a gramophone with a huge trumpet, and before it an elderly couple dressed entirely in black. He turned the radio off in disgust.

Sunday night: the end of a week, a sadness which was, he thought, a lot like dying. Streets empty, houses dark, the radio dead. He closed his eyes and then he heard, far away, the dismal whistle of the Galloping Goose. With a shiver he tried to think of Monday morning, and another day during which there was absolutely nothing–not a thing–that he *had* to do. He rolled over, pulled his knees up against his chest and shivered with pleasure at the prospect of being indolent for another long day. He tried to not hear the trolley's insistent whistle, which was like a call out of the blackness.

At the Khyber Pass

"Kill for Kali!" Apples rained off the tin breastworks, and one smashed through the wooden slats. "Kill for the love of Kali !"

"Smash the buggers," Chris cried, affecting a British accent. "Fire a volley." He threw the dirt clods overhand, saw them explode against Horace's fort like .303 bullets; in the darkness the dust floated away. "Bring up the Gatlin' gun!" More clods, more apples, the firing relentlessly exchanged from both sides until Chris was hit in the ribs and fell into his hole; the pain was intense but short-lived.

"Charge!" Horace shouted. "Drive out the English devils."

Chris was on his feet, shouting "Charge" and at the same time giving an imitation of a bugle. He grabbed a handful of young corn stalks and ran around his fort, throwing as he cleared it; a stalk sailed through the night with the force of a spear and hit him in the leg. He faltered, then was on his feet, throwing, rousing his troops by his own example; his corn stalk sped true, and was averted only at the last second as Horace jumped back.

"O it's Din Din Din," he cried. "Though I've belted you and flayed you."

"I'll flay you, English dog," Horace cried. "I'll draw and quarter you, and hang you from the ramparts." He threw his cornstalks in rapid succession, and when they were both empty-handed they fell to the ground, laughing, exhausted by the battle and the long day.

Tag

The smell of tar was overwhelming! He lay with his cheek against the edge of the roof and looked down into the street. His eyes strained against the blackness–the carless curbs, stark sidewalks, dark windows–and then in the dim neon of the intersection he saw a figure run. It was silhouetted against Reilly's Tavern briefly and then dropped into shadows. Chris watched, the odor of tar as black as night. Barely breathing, he listened.

How different the common sidewalks of Lents looked from this angle. He could almost imagine himself walking them year after year. Every crack or space had an association in his mind, and as he peered through the darkness at the silent street he tried to imagine seeing himself walking the sidewalk in some previous time, toward home or school, in any weather.

Now the streets were empty except for an occasional car; only the lights from the taverns and the Mt. Scott drugstore fell in muted squares. Yet he knew that somewhere in the darkness Martin, Harlan, Mal, and the others were hiding from whoever was It.

The game had begun casually about an hour earlier, and during that time they had chased each other over the roofs of Lents, from the Goodwill store all the way to the old Lents School. Never had their games covered such space, over such strange terrain. There were doorways and alleys, old trailers and empty cars, places they had never noticed became hiding places. Chris had been chased by someone clear from the Safeway store, and running like crazy he had rounded the fire station and headed for the stairs beside the Masonic Lodge. He went straight to the roof and lay on his back, gasping for breath. The odor of tar was a reminder of how hot the day had been; it boiled up into the night. Then he opened his eyes, looked into the blackness until the minute perforations slowly became perceptible one by one and he became aware of the galaxy swirling beyond the layer of darkness.

Now he watched the street until his eyes ached. When two figures stumbled around the corner by the old Rexall he thought they were drunks headed for Reilly's, but they went on past. Then the figure he had seen stepped out of the shadows by Menashe's fruit store, and another crossed under the flashing red stop light of the intersection; the four continued in Chris's direction and walked on past. What the hell? he wondered, and stood up as they walked in front of the lights of Jacobson's furniture store.

He ran carefully across the roof and down the wooden fire escape; the others were past the fire station when he started across the parking lot.

"Where you been, boah?" Martin asked, hitching up his pants. The others seemed not to notice him, and Chris felt left out–they would have gone home without him, he might have stayed on that roof all night.

"Couldn't find me, could ya?"

No one answered; they were listening to Mal. "Hells bells, it's just over the fence. Easy as cutting butter with a hot knife. Anyone comes we just drop it and run like hell." They were at the corner; Mal reached into the darkness and pulled up a long stalk of grass which he began to chew on. Across the street was Mac's grocery, the Oly and Blitz signs glowing in the window; across the street the other way, tall and gloomy, was the old Lents School.

"I'll go over and hand it out," Mal said. They crossed the street in a bunch and stood quietly beside the weathered lattice fence at the rear of the store. Mal grabbed the top boards and deftly pulled himself over; he hit the ground on the other side with a muffled noise. Chris watched the empty street, the flat blackness of the school front rising like a ghostly facade. Bottles rattled, and a case of pop rested on the fence. Martin and Harlan reached up, took a side, and carrying it knee-high they began to run easily around the corner and up 92nd.

Chris waited, scared, excited, feeling perhaps some sense of perverse loyalty toward Mal until he was on this side of the fence again, and then, his heart pounding with excitement and fear and pleasure, he began running. Ahead the bottles clinked faintly. They ran along the empty sidewalk, under an arc light and then quickly into the blackness; the street was deserted, and although it was only about ten o'clock most houses were dark. They ran into Lents Park and fell to the ground under the tall firs, the sense of the chase coursing through muscles. Chris gasped for breath, overwhelmed by the odor of fir needles and moss and the dark, damp earth of the park. Small globes of light swirled near the wading pool, and on the upper level near the empty tennis courts. A car came slowly down 92nd and their noisy breathing grew quiet until it passed. By the dim yellow headlights they knew it was not the police.

"They're all Squirt," Mal said, uncapping one bottle against another. The bottles had been agitated by the long run and they fizzed violently, filling the air with the scent of citrus juice. Chris tipped the bottle against his lips: the pop was warm.

"That was slick," Mal said, wiping his mouth with the back of his hand. "We could get two or three cases—sell what we don't drink." Mal always had a scheme; he knew where the fruit trees were and when the fruit was ripe, which basements had jars of home-made dill pickles, where groves of bamboo grew. He knew when people were home or were gone, and what might be worth taking. Chris had seen him walk into an open garage and take a handful of wrenches, and once he had taken a rug from a clothesline.

Harlan said that he and Verlyn had gone jockey-boxing the night before and had got a carton of cigarettes; then they had syphoned gas for Jergen's car. Mal said that he had hawked four squirt guns and a jeweled Duncan yo-yo at Stella's Variety. Harlan smiled and sort of scoffed.

Chris said, "What we ought to do is roll a drunk." He said it partly to impress the others, but also because he could see the scene so clearly: a drunk comes out of Reilly's Tavern and when he passes the alley they make a noise; he comes in to investigate and someone hits the drunk on the head right behind the ear very carefully. Chris was certain that he could duplicate the kind of blow he had seen in films and comic books; even now his pointer finger played over the surface of the raised area behind his ear. He would wrap a piece of pipe with friction tape, or fill a leather pouch with buckshot. Zow! Cloud Nine. He had played the scene over and over in his mind, and it seemed so *possible!*

The Manure Magnet

The noon whistle sounded from Dwyer's Mill.

From where he lay under the grove of fir trees Chris studied the dust motes which travelled slow currents through sun slats. Beside him Knight Street was a dusty, bumpy trail; here the air had a strong pitch smell, and all around the hot sun cooked up the odor of golden grass.

There was absolutely nothing that he *had* to do. Beside him Horace chewed on a stalk of grass, pondering the infinity of blue sky beyond the trees. There were things they *could* do: go home and eat lunch, read magazines, ride to Lents and read magazines, pick apples in the neighbor's yard–perhaps start an apple fight with the Woodruff Brothers.

Chris raised himself on an elbow, looked across the empty fields of brown and golden grass, and saw that Foster Road was empty of traffic. He listened: there was the echo of the noon whistle at the mill; briefly, the sound of a Hyster, and then nothing. He listened harder: a small cricket, Oregon Grape leaves rasping, a distant bird. The world seemed empty.

Where was everyone? He imagined Buzz hanging around the store, and Martin and Harlan ogling the girls at Mt. Scott pool; Mal was perhaps behind his father's garage smoking, or scouting the neighborhood for pickles to steal. Lents would be enjoying its brief mid-day bustle as workers emerged for lunch, and then it would fall into its usual doldrums. There was probably nothing happening anywhere.

He lay back in the warm grass, hands behind his head.

They could return to what they had been doing, working on their soap box racers, but the project involved so much effort. Horace had had the foresight to build his from lightweight materials–a white sheet stretched over a plywood framework–but Chris's was incredibly heavy. It seemed to take most of a day to haul the heavy racer over the rutted roads from his house to Foster, and to pull it through gravel until they were finally at the top of the 112th Street Hill. Dust churned, the sun beat down, the rope cut into his shoulder until he felt like a slave working on the great pyramid of Egypt. All that work for a few seconds of free-flight down the mountain!

A screen door slammed and Chris looked in that direction, saw a man disappear into the gardening area where poles supported green beans. Chris had the idea that that was some relative of Horace's.

"What's he do?" Chris asked, wondering why the man wasn't at work .

"Manure," Horace said, giggling, eyes closed against the sky. "He made his money on manure. He's a manure magnate."

"Magnet?" Chris asked; he had never heard the word used that way before.

Horace laughed, and rolled on his side. "That's right, he's a manure magnet," he said, laughing so hard that Chris began to laugh too, and this was the only sound in the entire neighborhood.

Hubcapping

He squinted at the street lights until they were starry blurs, and when he moved his head from side to side the blurs rotated amorphously. A little to his left and slightly behind Martin and Nancy walked; he could hear their close whispers. Perhaps they were talking about Donna, who was Nancy's best friend. He wanted to say that he *liked* Donna a lot but he couldn't. It was impossible to talk with girls, and that was one reason he walked slightly apart from Martin and Nancy, showing off just enough to call attention to himself but not enough to be terribly obvious about it.

At the roar of an open exhaust, the squeal of tires, he turned to see Martin and Nancy move apart, and Martin's arm drop from her shoulders. Two dim headlights came around the corner and the car roared toward them, forcing them off the road. A flash illuminated the houses like a flare as the car backfired and braked to a stop. Chris, figuring it was the Lents Gang, was prepared to run.

"Hay Jergens," Martin said. "How ya doing, boah?"

The car was old, with wooden spoke wheels and signs painted on the fenders and sides, like cars in Harold Teen. *Shot rod* and *Your daughter was hurt in this wreck* and 23 *Skidoo*. He didn't really know Jergens but he knew the jokes about Jergen's Lotion.

They stood at the edge of the road as the car pumped out a growing cloud of light blue smoke; then the door opened and Martin and Nancy climbed in. He hesitated, the door waited, and Martin called, "Well, c'mon, boah! Shag ass!" Almost without conscious movement he stepped to the runningboard and then was on the front seat, as the door closed with a thud. Jergens pulled the shift lever beside his leg, and the car shot into the night, the headlights barely denting the darkness.

How different from his father's car! Exciting noises rose from the engine, transmission, the underneath, and there was a darkness that seemed almost sinister. In the dim light from the instruments he could barely see the outline of Jergen's face reflected in the windshield: the long head, heavy chin, deep-set eyes.

Jergens spun the wheel, threatening to tip the car. Chris gripped the door edge in terror, and felt something hit his foot. He saw the glint of a beer bottle as it rolled across the floor. He smelled the sharp odor of gas, oil blowby, old upholstery, and he felt certain that he would die in this car, a headline.

Jergens raced through the dark streets and Chris thought how strange it was to see his neighborhood from this angle; houses he had seen for years were like strangers. They drove down his street, past his house, and as if in slow motion he saw the light in the front room, his father reading in the chair by the window, someone moving in the kitchen. There was time to see his father turn and peer through the screen at the car that raced past, and in that ponderous second Chris felt certain that his father had had time to study the car and its occupants.

"I'm getting me a car," Martin said, leaning forward until his chin rested on his arms on the back of the front seat; he shouted over the car's noises. "Next summer I'll get it." That was news to Chris, and he wondered where Martin would get the money. "How long've you had this one?" Martin asked.

"This one?" Jergens said, his voice echoing each syllable up through the cavern of his throat. Chris could not believe that Jergens was only a year older than he was. Jergens laughed and said, "Oh, about an hour."

The beer bottle rolled to the other side, hit the transmission hump, and slowly Chris began to suspect that the car was stolen.

Once on his paper route he had come upon an accident at the Galloping Goose tracks. A long, black sedan had been hit by the trolley, and it lay on its top, doors agape. The casualties had been taken away, but the trail of oil, dark blood on the pavement, the empty bottle that rolled on the inverted roof created a mood of anarchy that he could not forget. That was how he felt now, as they raced through the dark streets, and he gripped his own knees tightly with both hands as an excited fear shook through his legs. He wanted to say Stop, let me out, and yet with the same breath to say, Faster, faster!

Jergens roared down 103rd to Foster, and swung left. After the brilliance of the PGE sub-station, there was the glow of the end-of-the-line bus turnaround, the bounce of the trolley tracks, and the dimness of the Last Chance tavern; after that there was only the darkness of the countryside. The tallow yellow headlights vibrated along the road, the underside growled, a fender or exhaust pipe rattled; in the backseat Martin and Nancy whispered, and beside him Jergens drove with deliberation to some unknown place. No one knew where he was! He imagined his parents opening a newspaper to learn of his death. All of his mother's warnings, all the vague images of Boogie-Town, the strange lives behind the illustrations of the movie page in the paper, the rough men alluded to as "kidnappers" came together with sudden clarity.

Jergens slowed at 136th, stopped, cut his lights. They waited, and he said, "Some caps up there. Grab a couple." He handed something over the backseat and Chris felt a long screwdriver dropped in his lap. He couldn't find the words to refuse, and then they were moving slowly forward without lights, the car's exhaust thumping against the darkness of the fir trees. Near the service station was the car, black against the night; as they got closer Chris could see it was a newish Cadillac. Jergens stopped and as Chris looked at the empty road Martin pushed the seat forward. "C'mon, boah," he whispered, then jumped past him. He squatted at the nearest wheel; there was the sound of metal being wrenched.

Chris hesitated, jumped out and ran around the parked car; he slipped the screwdriver under the chrome disc and pried back. The noise grated against his ears, louder than he could have imagined–it was the sound of gravel rattled in a can, of an angry cat, a roller skate on pavement. He hesitated, listened, then slid the screwdriver under the other side; the hubcap wrenched loose, fell to the ground and rolled in a never-ending circle. He fumbled, tried to hold the hubcap down with both hands to silence it. Grabbing the heavy hubcap, he ran to the car just as Martin reached it, and they struggled side by side. A dog barked, and he thought he heard a door open, voices, and then Martin was falling over the seat as Jergens stepped on the gas. Chris ran beside the car, jumped in, and pulled the door shut. His legs were shaking and he realized that he had left the screwdriver back there on the ground–with his fingerprints on it!

Vision

The hour is pre-dawn, that time when the sky's grayness is intense and temporary. Yet he is certain that the light is always like this and that the sun will not come up–this moment will be forever.

He is inside a building which seems to be a house but the rooms stretch into darkness. The furniture is dark, heavy, elaborate: the long divan upholstered in deep purple velvet, the marble tabletop, the ornate lamps with fringed shades and tassels. The floors extend like mirrors toward the walls, as if this space is used for dancing. The intense gray light comes from the tall windows, which are flanked by heavy drapes and columns which rise into the darkness above.

The windows are actually a series of doors, and he goes through the opening; the marble floor extends to a balcony without interruption, and he walks to the cement balustrade. There is a wide brick stairway to the lower level, and at each end of the railing a pair of marble urns, which lend a funereal air to the scene. The lawn is flat and flawless, bordered on all sides by immaculate, mature cypress trees which scribe the gray sky like brush strokes. He is struck by the solitude, the silence, the stasis.

Jockey-Boxing

They waited in their bags, the sky beyond the trees growing darker as throughout the neighborhood light after light was extinguished. Radios droned to silence. In every house fathers turned off the Molle Mystery Theater and hit the pillow with sad exhaustion. A last car passed, a slow whizz of tires.

The summer sky rolled with stars; the air was charged with the perfume of late lilac, wisteria, pine pitch. The smells were dark as shadows, and Chris lay in his bag, unable to sleep, arms folded beneath his head, staring straight up at the stars which pulsed nearer. Patiently he waited, drunk on the smell of fresh cut grass.

Martin said, "Okay, boah, let's go." He crawled from the sleeping bag, slipped into pants and shoes, and followed across the lawn. In the shadows beside the house, where Martin's parents slept, they moved cautiously, tennis shoes padding across the gravel. Beyond the house he felt excitement pound in his chest, becoming a giggle he could barely hold.

Quickly they walked down the street, away from the arc light, and cut across the field until they came to the pavement. Under the huge firs' shadows they surveyed the street: a new Chevy convertible, top down. But it sat in the umbrella of light from the house, and Martin said that he saw someone on the porch. They waited, hearing the sound of their own breath.

Although it was past ten, he wasn't sleepy. In the mossy shadows the air was charged with a lazy perfume; the summer moon sailed the clear sky. How strange to be out this late, in this night world; as he watched the dark street he felt a surge of excitement. He had not done this kind of thing last summer—how quickly things change, he thought. Already Martin, who was a year older, was beginning to shave. Would he, he wondered, next year?

"Watchit, boah," Martin said. Lights swept the street, a beacon's finger. The car turned the corner and halfway down the block found a driveway; they heard the car door slam, then a screen door.

They waited until the house lights went out.

He could feel the pine needles against his palms, smell their rich odor. They crouched behind the laurel hedge, their faces framed by the oily leaves, until the house lights went out, and then he followed Martin into the shadows beside the car, his heart bursting against ribs. The car window was still rolled down, and now there was only the matter of the possible light in the jockey-box—some had it, some didn't.

He heard the click, heard Martin running his fingers through the man's life: the rustle of a map, fuses, screws. He heard or thought he heard a noise from the house—the man rolling over his wife, raising himself from her to perhaps reach into the drawer for a pistol. When Martin said, "Let's go, boah," he exhaled the breath he didn't realize he had been holding, and they were running into the yawning darkness of the field, toward Martin's house.

"Got some smokes, and a damn good knife," Martin said, when they were safely home. Martin laid the bone-handled knife beside the crumpled pack of Luckies. Once they had got a pint of whiskey; another time a pair of binoculars.

They lay on top of their bags, debating whether to look for another car to jockey-box, and finally decided to have a cigarette. Chris took one, put it to his lips, felt the harsh tobacco. Martin had the matches out when the light flashed on in the house next door—his own house. He saw a shadow pass the window, and supposed it was his father headed toward the bathroom. He put the cigarette down and crawled into the open mouth of the sleeping bag, waiting against sleep until that light went out and the entire neighborhood dropped into darkness.

White River

He sat on the front steps and looked at the star-filled sky, surprised and pleased to be here: in the house his parents and sister slept; the entire silent street was asleep. He could see only one house light, several blocks away. Because there was not even an arc light nearby to diminish the darkness the stars were brilliant–they conjured an image of the sands of time, of the desert, pyramids, and Chris felt dizzy when he tried to imagine how they spread to infinity.

He followed the trail of stars downward, until they merged with the string of red lights on the radio tower on Mt. Scott, near The Point. Below the tower the mountain was a dark mass without an opening. Again he looked up and down the dark street, surprised to be sitting on his porch at this hour and all the rest of the neighborhood asleep. Last night he had set his alarm for 3:30, and he had worried that he would not wake up in time.

He heard the sound of tires on gravel, saw the headlight beams sweep the trees, and finally the car turned the corner. Chris got up, gathered his gear, and was waiting on the street when the car pulled to a stop. Horace opened the rear door and Chris threw in his knapsack and canteen; he climbed in back, cradling his rifle on his knees. Horace's father put the car in gear and slowly they moved down the deserted street, the Chev's transmission whine breaking the stillness. They turned the corner, passed Buzz's house, passed all the sleeping neighborhood as they travelled down Harold heading east.

"Pretty early," Chris said.

"Getting a good start," Horace's father said.

"Hmmmmph," Horace said.

Their voices were blurred with sleep; they exchanged a few words and then were silent. Horace's father kept his speed at thirty-five until they were on Powell; he raised it to forty, except for the minute it took to get through Gresham, and then they sailed eastward at a blazing forty-five mph. Inwardly, Chris groaned with impatience–they'd never get there at this speed–but as soon as they had left Portland they were in the country and now past Gresham they were in the wilds. The texture of the air seemed different–thinner, cleaner, loaded with the sharp odor of evergreen. He loved to get into the woods, and as they drove he studied the fields that became woods which soon became forests, darker than the night.

Horace's father talked about how he used to hunt rabbits in Eastern Oregon with bow and arrow. Chris saw him as an English archer–he looked very British, with a long jaw and slightly wavy hair. Chris liked to hear the stories, and he felt cozy in the car with the dash lights reflecting against the windshield. He longed to hunt, to live totally in the wilderness and to be so independent that he wouldn't need to buy anything, except perhaps bullets. He imagined at times how in case of atomic attack he would take to the woods. He would be ready, and there was no doubt in his mind that he could live well with the barest margin of comfort.

In Sandy light came from a cafe window, and Chris could see the woman inside wiping off an empty counter. They drove on, the engine pumping a steady beat, toward the horizon which emerged in the false dawn. Past Brightwood and Zigzag, the river a fast white glow in the dark forest. They had seen only two other cars since Gresham. Past Rhododendron, and the engine began to strain against the incline.

Mt. Hood was a dark monolith raised against the lighter sky, its craggy sides beginning to glow a pinkish-blue. Horace's father shifted into second gear, and the engine whined upward, to where the road teetered above sheer cliffs. As they neared Government Camp they came over a rise and there against the horizon was the tip of sun, a brilliant orange; below them the entire valley was stippled with light. Chris felt his breath go out at the sight of this beauty.

Then they were heading down the eastern slope, back into the forest; Horace's father left the car in second gear and continued to brake occasionally, to curb their descent. Through the dense forest Chris could see snow melt-off cascading downhill, gathering in pools, becoming small waterfalls. He looked for deer, or perhaps a bear or a cougar. His dream was to build a small cabin in a place like this, to hunt, trap, and fish for a living, smoking meat, growing some vegetables, making homebrew, and during the long winter evenings to sit before the fireplace reading.

The road flattened, and they headed into the desert, toward the rising sun. The land was flat and barren except for sagebrush and a few stunted juniper trees; there were no houses, farms, or even fences. Then they turned off the paved road and drove slowly along a narrow, graveled road, the car raising a plume of dust, until they came to White River. The sun-covered stones which indicated the rim of the canyon sprang at them from the barren landscape; they were at the edge, teetering on the dirt road which snaked toward the river at the canyon's bottom. When Chris opened the window he smelled the air, still crisp, loaded with the scent of sagebrush and juniper. He gripped his rifle more tightly, expecting to see a rabbit or ground squirrel.

The car began to slowly descend the narrow road that wound downward. In the shadow of the rim-rock the air was chilly, and Chris trembled–partly in anticipation of the hunt–and then they crossed the plank bridge which spanned the swift water and were in sunlight again. The Chevy groaned upward in low gear and Chris pressed his face against the warm glass to look straight down at the river.

When they got to the top of the north rim, Horace's father parked the car and they got out. Chris breathed deeply and exhaled–the air was sharp, carried on the breeze from the Cascades, but soon the day would be blazing hot. Chris had his clip loaded; he inserted it but left the chamber empty. He took his canteen, hunting knife, and a small four-power telescope; these he hooked on his belt.

They walked toward the boulders which were the canyon walls, keeping a sharp eye for rattlesnakes. Horace scanned the rocks with the scope on his rifle, and Chris looked through the telescope; he could see the small gray animals running nimbly among the rocks but the distance was too great for the .22's.

As they walked along the rim a ground squirrel dashed toward a rock outcrop about fifty feet away; Chris swung the bolt back and cocked the rifle, bringing a shell into the chamber, and almost without sighting he fired from the shoulder. A plume of dust rose beyond the squirrel, and again when Horace shot. Chris slid the bolt back, smelled the pleasant odor of cordite and oil, and drove home another shell; he aimed just ahead of the target, squeezed the trigger, heard the flat crack, heard the zing of the bullet sailing off into the desert, heard Horace's rifle, and saw the squirrel dive into its burrow. They started to laugh, talking about how close their shots had come, how for a second the desert's stillness had overtones of a fine battle; these were the stories they'd tell each other in the coming weeks.

They slipped their rifles on safety, and held them at the ready as they advanced along the rimrock, the whole day stretching before them like the open countryside.

The Ground Squirrels

"Dammit, Chris," Fowlick said. "If you can't stop them from pissing on the stove we'll just have to find someone who can." He was only four or five years older, but he was staring hard at Chris, like a father. "You want to be Branch Manager but you can't keep order here."

"I told them not to," Chris said, then stopped, not trusting the quiver in his voice. He felt tears well at the back of his eyes.

"You told them," Fowlwick said. "But they pissed on the stove, and when the morning route came this place smelled like a toilet. It was awful. Now, if that happens again, you're through." He looked at him hard. Chris saw the small specks of whiskers on the Fowlwick's pink cheeks; saw the cigarette come to his mouth, the smoke spew out. "You got that?"

"Yeah," he said, unable to say more. He continued folding his papers, and when enough time had passed so that he felt he wasn't under scrutiny he went out and got his paper bag from his bike. How was he supposed to stop them if they insisted on building a roaring fire and then pissing on it? What could he do? Fight them? But the job of Branch Manager paid $4.65 a month, and he wanted the money.

When he took the bag from his handlebars he felt the weight of the ground squirrels. He had brought them to show to the other kids; the squirrels were stiff and bloated, already swelling in the heat. He picked up a carcass, his nose turning away at the thick odor of blood and fur, and started to toss it away. On impulse he swung it in a circle by the tail–thinking of how King Cambyses captured Pelusium by hurtling dead cats over the walls–and let it fly. It fell on the flat roof of the branch office. He tossed the other two up, and when he thought of them decaying, rotting, becoming bleached skeletons in this secret place he was pleased.

Oxblood

The new leather absorbed the liquid like a blotter, and he saw it turn from natural brown to a beautiful red; in places there was an iridescent glow, like oil on water. He loved the strong smell of the dye and new leather, and turned the shoe in his hand so that the surface caught the sunlight.

He had spent as much for this pair of genuine English Brogues as his parents had spent for any three pair of shoes they had bought for him. They had objected, but it was his paper route money, and finally they had said, "Well, if you really want them." Of course he wanted them–he had to have them, all the high school kids would have them. He had seen the older boys on the bus and in the drugstore with their highly polished oxblood or cordovan brogues, each trying to out-do the others to achieve a perfect mirror-like surface, and he had seen the Boomer Boys on Broadway standing under the dazzling neon of the theater marquees, polishing one shoe and then the other on the back of their pants leg until the cords took on a reddish color.

He had never paid much attention to his clothes. He had spent a lot of time grooming his hair–alternating between a crewcut and another style which combined a high wave in front with a duck's ass in back–and once, when Harlan started a trend, he had talked his mother into giving him a Toni curl and bleaching the ends. But generally he wore Levis and a work shirt, and he might wear the same clothes for a whole week without noticing whether they were dirty or torn.

But now that he was starting high school he knew, by looking around and talking with some of the sharper kids, that there were certain things that he needed. His list far exceeded his funds: a pair of Day's cream cords, a pair of Levi's, two striped dress shirts with cutaway collars, a blue hidden-button shirt, three pair of argyle socks, and a narrow, half rounded leather belt like the other kids wore. He had bought a pair of suntan pants–not the popular brand, but a pair of work pants, heavy, harsh–which he had had his mother streamline by pegging the legs to a narrow taper, slimming the cuff, and sewing down the belt loops.

He loved shopping for clothes–loved the smell of the stores, the rows of bright cloth, the textures of corduroy and cashmere, the silver flecked sheen of new Levi's, the unblemished surface of leather. In the store there was a sense of optimism and a view of the future which suggested: if you wear good clothes everything will be all right. The store dummies all carried brief cases, as if headed for school and the good jobs. When he had tried on the brogues he felt taller, and secure in the way the new leather gripped his ankles. He saw high school as the chance to make a new start, and he secretly told himself that he would change his ways, quit fooling around, and that he would succeed.

When the dye had dried, he laid on another coat, working his way carefully from the upturned toe and around the heavy seams to the back. The soles, which were an inch thick, he did last. He had taken the shoes directly from the store to the shoe repair shop and had had them half-soled, with an inset cleat added to the heel.

He began to brush the leather, bringing the dye to a dull shine. Then with another brush he applied the paste polish, working it carefully into the grain. He put the shoe on his foot, extended the toe over the edge of the porch, and began to use the soft cloth; he held an end in each hand and sawed the cloth quickly across the leather, until it blazed in the sunlight. He could actually see the fuzzy image of his face in the triangular toe! He applied another coat of polish, and spit on the shoe; when he swiped the rag across it a few times the color was brilliant, and he knew why they called this polish oxblood.

The Stink

"What in hell stinks around here?" Fowlwick said, walking to the doorway and looking out. He lit a cigarette and absently polished the toe of a shoe against the back of his pant leg. "God, smell it? It's awful!"

"What's it smell like?" Chris asked, barely able to keep from laughing.

"It's terrible," Fowlwick said, clearing his throat and spitting into the street. "It's like somebody took a dump in here, or something. "

A crazy kid named Scarz looked up from the stack of papers he was folding. "Yeah," he said, "I been smelling something too for about a week."

"What is it," Burton said, "your mother's panties?" Everyone laughed except Fowlwick, who perhaps felt that Scarz had not helped his cause. "Anybody else smell it?" he asked. Chris began to stack his folded papers into the bag, so that he could keep his face down as he tried to stifle the laughter that welled within.

Negatives

They picked through the ashes, looking for anything which could have survived a fire which had virtually leveled the house. Part of the fireplace remained, the end of a trail of bricks spread across the lawn. A charred bathtub and toilet were upended, bedsprings were already beginning to rust. Horace found a flagpole holder which he thought he could use in his room, and Chris found an interesting bottle; otherwise there was nothing of value.

The house had stood in the wide yard across from Lents Park, facing 92nd. Chris had always thought that this was one of the most impressive houses he had ever seen. Tall and graceful, it sat well back from the road, down a driveway flanked with tall firs; the windows were latticed and had heavy shutters that worked. A balcony on the second floor overlooked the circular drive enclosing a flower garden. The house was huge, yet it was dwarfed by the tall firs, and Chris had often tried to imagine what it would be like to live in that house on a stormy October night.

The night before the house had burned, and there were rumors that the old woman who had lived there for years had set it afire. Chris imagined her on the balcony, silhouetted against the flames, her black dress becoming brittle in the intense heat, laughing perhaps before the house crashed around her.

In back there was a small garage, its latticed windows and cedar shake roof untouched by the fire, and they pulled their wagon to its door. They found two sets of deer antlers, a stack of National Geographics, a 1934 Sears catalogue, an old automobile horn, and two picture frames; they put these into the wagon, but threw away a box of old letters and post cards. There was a plaster globe with the continents barely outlined, a stack of yellowed newspapers, a broken lawnmower, a tire. All these they left.

Then on a workbench, covered with cobwebs, they found a wooden box and opened it to uncover rows of six inch square glass plates. Chris took out one and held it up to the light; as he turned it he could see a faintly etched picture of the Columbia River Gorge, with mountains in the background. Another showed a couple standing beside a tall touring car, and a third showed a family in a field.

"Take them," Horace said. "We'll use them for targets." They loaded everything in the wagon and pulled it down the sidewalk toward home. At the corner they met Teddy Gaff and Dick Issari, who looked at the junk and shook their heads.

"Why'd you want that?" Dick asked, his fat round face serious and puzzled.

"This is good stuff," Chris said, and Horace laughed, slightly uncomfortable.

"Yeah? What the hell you going to do with it?"

"We might sell it," Chris said, "or trade with the Barth Brothers. Who knows?"

"Man," Teddy said, folding his big arms against his chest, "when you guys going to grow up?"

Quitting the Route

When he had folded and bagged all his papers he had to wait until Donnie and Ike, the two new boys, had finished folding theirs. They moved with incredible slowness, the bulky paper too large for their hands; they'll learn, Chris thought. How long ago was it that he had been green at it? he wondered, thinking back over a long year and every day, every day except Sunday (that big fat edition was delivered the night before), the insistence of the route.

He picked up some strands of wire and wove them into a continuous piece; standing on the sidewalk, he swung the wire and threw it over the electric bus trolleys: one last time.

Finally, after Donnie and Ike had wheeled off unsteadily in different directions, Chris quickly swept out the branch office and locked the door: that was that. The next time he'd see the yellow building he would be an outsider, a visitor; he'd know the same feeling he had felt when he had gone to the branch in the grayness of dawn to accompany Buzz on his morning route. There had been a different bunch of carriers, and he felt that the grates on the windows had been put there to keep him out.

He pedaled slowly down Foster toward Lents, stopped at the Siberian ice cream store for a cone to celebrate this last circuit, then rode past the Lents library and around the corner and up 92nd.

At Harold his route began: past Lents park, hitting each porch that was his, feeling a sense of satisfaction as the bag lightened imperceptibly. That was *that* one, and *that* one:

Johnson, Marstoni, Parsons, Krutsinger. They were more than names in a phone book; some customers he had got by walking door to door until he was exhausted. He had never won any of the *Oregonian's* subscription-drive prizes (did they actually send a newsboy to Pasadena to see the Rose Bowl, or was it the editor's son? he wondered), although he had twice gone to Jantzen Beach with Buzz for the paper's picnic. Buzz was proof that you had to be dishonest to win. He signed up dozens of unknowing customers, delivered the paper for a few days, until he had collected a prize, and then stopped delivery. Chris knew that there was no getting ahead without strategy.

He rode to Holgate, where his route ended, and turned around. Holgate was being dug up from 82nd to 92nd, to be paved and widened. Chris remembered when he had had a *Shopping News* route, and had had to carry three bags of papers, one on the handlebar and two over the back fender; Holgate had narrowed to a rutted, dirt road and often when he had shot down the hill, bouncing at every bump, the front wheel trapped in the rut, paper bags flying, he had been out of control.

He pedaled easily down 92nd, enjoying the sidewalk.

Across the street the landscape from the hill to Holgate looked like a war-zone; they were moving houses in order to expand Lents Park. He tried to imagine their tiny park getting that big, and he hoped that they'd put in a swimming pool so that Lents people wouldn't have to continue feeling inferior to Mt. Scott people.

At Steele he left the sidewalk for the rest of the route: now it was blacktop and unpaved, bumpy roads. He passed The Path, got all houses above the hill, weaving back and forth until he got to 99th, dropped down to Harold, and worked his way back to 93rd. Now he was in his immediate neighborhood, the few blocks he had known all his life, where every stone and bush wore the casual air of familiarity: he waved to people who had been neighbors and friends before they had been customers.

Here was Buzz's house, comfortably nestled under the huge English walnut tree, and Orlando's grocery store, already illuminated although it was not dark. The odor of a hundred dinners cooking carried on the warm air and he pedaled lazily, thinking of the people in their houses who carried on their private lives while waiting for the *plop* of his paper on that porch.

He came down Reedway, his street, hitting a house on one side and then cutting across to the other; past Bob Mountain's house and Bill Ford's one-room shack, where he did not leave papers, past Yeaman's and Martin's, where he did. And then to his own house: the bike rolling easily he reached into the bag and with a fluid motion threw the tightly-rolled paper overhand. It sailed through the air to land squarely on the porch without hitting window, bush or screen door . He pedaled away, saw his mother in the kitchen, heard the front room radio grow fainter.

The road abruptly became bumpy dirt. His wheels flowed over the ruts, the bag became lighter. As the road got worse, the houses became smaller, more dingy, hidden behind thick trees or stuck out on a barren yard like a sore thumb. Heller, Tippy, Peebles (who was impossible to collect from) all wanted and got what their lives needed: news of murders, foreign wars, accidents, the fantasy of comics, the prospects of the classifieds, the promise of the weather report.

The roads at times were little more than trails among the fields of tall grass, Oregon Grape, and Scotch Broom. Past Horace's house (an exception among the junky places), up Yukon to 103rd to Harold again and then he wended his way along the road which outlined this edge of the swamp-the very last houses in this part of Portland, cut off, he imagined, from civilization except for the news which he brought. Around 104th street to Nelson's house, down the twin ruts to the tarpaper shack behind the tavern; he slid the paper into the box and pedaled away from the darkness of greasy machinery, black earth. He had never seen the man, always got his money from a hand which reached around the opaque screen door. Apparently the guy was starting a junk yard, because parts of cars spilled out from his cluttered porch clear into the street.

He rode across Foster, where car lights were beginning to appear, and to 108th Street where he had six customers. The last house was at the end of the street, where it butted against the base of Mt. Scott. When he turned to begin the long ride back to Foster and toward home, he noticed that the sky had darkened into night; a single star appeared directly overhead.

He stopped at the bridge over Johnson Creek and watched the water trickle past. Music blared from the Last Chance tavern, and a car kicked gravel from the parking lot as it sped off toward Lents.

That was it: he had delivered his last paper. How did he feel, he wondered: good. He thought about the nuisance of having to stay home so that he could be available; now he could go places. He thought about the discomfort of delivering papers in winter, when a thin coat of ice would form on the bike's metal, or of riding through a wind-driven rain on these god-awful roads. Once his father's Lincoln had become stuck on 104th when he had taken Chris on the route, and they had worked for hours to free it. Some nights it had been fun, but mostly he remembered the dark, dreary nights of winter when the gray sky complemented his mood. It was over. Anyway, a guy in high school could find better ways to make money–paper routes were for kids.

He undid the paper-bag on the handlebar, removed the grip, and, tipping the bike, took from the handlebar a cigarette butt. He tasted tobacco, then lit it, inhaling deeply. He exhaled, looked at the ash. He had made enough money to buy some clothes for school–a pair of Levis, a pair of Day's yellow cords, two classy shirts, and a beautiful pair of English brogues. He was all right–and besides, if he needed money he could always find a job. Quitting, cutting off his income, made him slightly nervous, and he had quit mainly because his mother wanted him to do well in school; but the thought that there were other jobs comforted him.

He took another puff, felt his mind race with the excitement of all the possibilities the world ahead might hold, felt dizzy, felt his heart begin to pound. He flipped the butt into Johnson Creek, saw sparks flash, and as he pedaled toward home he realized: that's that.

The Last Battle

Chris dug the hole deeper, as if his life depended on it.

Ahead of the hole he had propped a large piece of corrugated tin, supported by broken tree limbs, and in the center of the tin he had poked a peep-hole half the size of a penny. Each end of the breastworks was blocked with boards and stacks of corn stalks, but the backside was open.

He dug the hole deeper and longer, making it into a short trench; the dirt was placed alongside for protection. When he had finished he stood back and admired it. It was a solid fort, and would withstand a strong barrage. A flag flew from the observation post, part of a sheet with the coat of arms stained in with berry juice. A large pile of dirt clods and apples were on the ramparts, cornstalks were stacked like lances at each end, and a sword and shield lay beside the hole.

Thirty feet away was Horace's fort, the tri-colour riding on the evening breeze. They had dug the holes earlier in the summer—it seemed so long ago now—on a day when they had had nothing better to do, and the skirmishes which had begun with a casual exchange of shots had grown into an all-out battle.

This one, with school only a week away, with a hint of fall in the air, would be their last.

The last battle, and the best: they dug their forts deeper, widened the holes into trenches, made the breastworks stronger, and their weaponry became more sophisticated. Fine road dust was scooped into tin cans and small paper bags. They folded coarser dust and gravel into flat newspaper packets, and left one side undone so the bomb would open upon impact. Laths were sharpened into broadswords, with smaller pieces added for the crossbar; garbage can lids became shields. Toward late afternoon they sat in the sun, laughing, punching holes in apples with a sharp stick, and placing a Zebra firecracker in each hole. It would be the battle for Constantinople, Thermopylae, the Franks and

Saracens matching blade for blade, the Tuarag Lancers defending a waterhole, the Crusaders leveling a town in the name of God: it was the history of warfare compressed into a few hours in this edge of the city field.

They met after dinner, the sun setting beyond their flags.

They checked armament, and then each warrior built a small fire. Chris built his to the far right of his ammunition, where it would be accessible but wouldn't blind or illuminate him. The wood smoke curled skyward a few feet and then the funnel cloud flattened, drifting casually into the space between their positions.

They waited.

The sun dropped and the sky became gray, then blue black; stars appeared one by one. Moonlight filtered through the tall fir trees at Chris's back, each limb glowing with a soft sheen. A car moved slowly down Foster Road, and turned left toward Dwyer's mill. When it was gone the field and the entire neighborhood was deathly still.

A dirt clod struck the top of the breastworks and exploded in a cloud of dust; at the same moment Chris heard Horace's imitation of a Mexican bugle and his shout: "No quarter! No quarter!" From his tiny observation hole Chris saw another clod hurtle past and heard it disappear in the bushes behind.

Chris shivered with excitement, and reached for an apple bomb; he had it lit, had his arm raised, when a paper sack struck the fort, spewing fine dust across his head and back. The apple bomb was thrown badly and went off somewhere on the ground. He coughed, fanned a space in the air, and lit another bomb. The wick sputtered as he touched it to a glowing ember in the bonfire, and burst into bright sparks as he threw it; he watched from the observation hole and saw it pass a newspaper gravel bomb, saw it travel down the trail of dust and explode over Horace's throwing hand. For a split second the flash lit the field.

"Assassin! " Horace cried.

A dust bomb left a vapor trail across the night and burst on the ground behind Chris.

"Dog! Eater of pork!"

"My bullets are dum-dums rubbed in pig fat!"

They alternated the exchange of apples and dustbombs, until the air was dense with smoke and dust. Through a haze the moonlight could barely penetrate Chris could see the glow of Horace's bonfire. The battle scene seemed so *real* that Chris jumped out of the hole and, rapid fire, threw a series of heavy dirt clods; they followed a steep arc and ended, he hoped, just beyond the barricades. He jumped into his hole in time to hear the *flatflugh* of an apple skim past. He trembled as he lit another apple bomb–this had two firecrackers, the wicks intertwined–and lobbed it overhead. From the peephole he saw two separate explosions flash through the sky.

"Cripes," Horace said, chuckling. "Christian devil!"

"Death to the infidel!"

They fired rapidly, exchanged bomb for bomb, rattling dirt clods across the barren ground, until Horace called that his ammo supply was gone.

"Tough," Chris shouted. "You called no quarter" He lit an apple bomb, held it until the fuse was partly burnt and lobbed the apple overhand.

"C'mon," Horace said, acting irritated. "You dope. Poor excuse for cannon fodder."

"Speak, O one about to die." Chris threw his last dust bomb, saw it spatter across Horace's fort, the dust rising with the smoke and the ghostly mist that was called from the low places. He grabbed his shield, jabbed the sword into the ground, and filled his hands with apples.

"Charge!" Chris yelled, the joy of battle sending a shiver across his back; he jumped from the hold, his shield close to his face, and he imitated a bugle's excited sound as he stepped around the bulwarks.

"Death to the infidels!" Horace screamed, his voice a Saracen trumpet. "Give no quarter! Show no mercy!" he screamed.

Through the darkness. Chris could barely see the figure moving away from the fire, and then he felt something strike his buckler. He held it closer, and the second blow sent a tremor down his arm. He began to pump apple after apple into the night; saw them float like tracers and disappear. Something hard struck his hip. The shield held near his face, he dropped back to pick up more apples when a cornstalk sailed from nowhere; it came down a greased slide of air, and his feet were moving so slowly it was impossible to dodge.

"Kill for the love of Kali!" Horace shouted, and Chris fired three apples at a place where the laugh trailed off Horace yelled, cursed, and Chris heard something spin past his head.

When the apples and dirt clods were gone they threw corn stalks, rushing together in a brief clash, throwing whatever they could pick up, fighting until the stalks were broken. Then they swung the dirt-covered end like a mace, laying into shields with a fury.

"Swords!" Chris shouted. "To arms! To arms!"

They laid into each other fiercely, blade rattling on buckler— slashing the garbage can lids with a wild frenzy until Horace, in a burst of enthusiasm, drove Chris backward into his own fort where he tripped, almost falling into the fire.

"Draw and quarter!" Horace screamed, waving his sword.

"Show no mercy. Spread-eagle the beggars to an ant-hill. Leave their eye-balls for the buzzards." Horace kicked apart Chris's fort, scattering dirt, wood, and sheet tin, and if there was any ultimate "victory" this was it.

Chris laughed and gasped for breath at the same time; he threw off his shield and lay back, sweat running down his face and arms smearing the coat of dust and ashes. Horace stood on the ruined bulwarks, the fire light playing against his blackened skin and clothes. His shirt was ripped across the front, and large dark splotches showed how terrible the battle had been. The air was filled with a fine layer of dust and wood smoke, and high above the dark towering fir trees Chris saw a full moon floating into the star-filled sky. He lay back, got his breath: the air had chilled noticeably, and the stars, glittering points of light, seemed much closer. He thought of the sands of the desert, of the pyramids, of eternity. The fire burned to embers, and he saw the moonlight' reflecting from every leaf. The fir trees were outlined against the full moon, serrated edges that evoked for Chris a timelessness, a time which perhaps had never been.

The battle was over, the neighborhood was suddenly quiet: a dog barked along the street, a tree frog began to croak, and far down the line he heard the Galloping Goose clacking against the rails.

About the Author

Albert Drake was born in Portland, Oregon when it was less populous and life had the quality of Norman Rockwell paintings. He was educated in public schools and followed his father's footsteps, working for years in service stations, garages and automotive warehouses. He eventually attended Portland State College, and got his degrees at the University of Oregon. He twice won the Ernest Haycox Prize for fiction. For nearly 30 years he labored in the groves of academe, where he was cited for his outstanding teaching and rose to the rank of Full Professor. He was the first academic to teach a class in science fiction as literature, and for several years he was Director of the Clarion Science Fiction Workshop. He has received numerous academic and creative grants, including two major grants from the National Endowment for the Arts. His fiction, poetry and prose have been widely published in literary quarterlies and popular magazines, including *Redbook*, *Epoch*, *North American Review* and *The Best American Short Stories*. He is currently Professor Emeritus of English.

Books by Albert Drake

Poetry
Michigan Signatures (Ed) (1969)
Riding Bike (1973)
Cheap Thrills (1975)
Rustfire (1975)
Returning to Oregon (1975)
Garage (1981)
Homesick (1988)

Fiction
The Postcard Mysteries (1975)
Tillamook Burn (1977)
In the Time of Surveys (1978)
I Remember the Day James Dean Died (1983)

Novels
One Summer (1979)
Beyond the Pavement (1981)

Non-Fiction
Street Was Fun in '51 (1982)
The Big "Little GTO" Book (1982)
A 1950's Rod & Custom Builder's Wishbook (1985)
Herding Goats (1989)
Hot Rodder!: From Lakes to Street (1993)
Flat Out (1994)
Fifties Flashback (1998)
Portland Pictorial: The 1950s (2006)
Northwest Oldtimers (2007)
Age of Hot Rods (2008)
Jacket & Plaque (2008)
Christmas at Ed's Richfield (2009)
Overtures to Motion (2011)

www.flatoutpress.com